Burden's Moon

The New Protectorate Stories: 2025 Holiday Special

Abigail Kelly

Author's Note

Burden's Moon is a short story collection set within the wider *New Protectorate Series* and is best enjoyed after reading the other books in the series. A full character directory can be found at abigailkkelly.com. Content warnings can also be found there, as well as in the backmatter of this book, alongside a glossary.

~Abigail

Full Series List

The New Protectorate:

Glow - novella
Astray - novella
Weathering - novella
Consort's Glory - novel
Empire - novella
Courtship's Conquest - novel
Strike - novella
Vital - novella
Burden's Bonds - novel
Kohl - holiday novella
Faraway - novella
Sanguine - novella
Devotion's Covenant - novel
Valor's Flight - novel
Burden's Moon - short story collection
Captive's Sentinel - novel

The New Protectorate Syndicate:

Grim's Delight - novel

The New Protectorate Fracture:

Splintered Vigil - novel

The United Territories and Allies

ESTABLISHED 1917

The United Territories and Allies
Current borders (2044) established
in the 1917 Peace Charter.

Member territories share a common currency and many laws, but maintain individual sovereignty. Each territory holds representation in the UTA Congress and Court, found in the United Neutral Zone.

Contents

A Guide to Burden's Moon 1
Ruffled Feathers Cafe 2
Solbourne Feast 10
Wilson Family Dinner 19
Pineridge Potluck 22
Empire Estate Celebrates 28
Princess Astrid Lights the Flame 32
Merfolk in the Moonlight 38
Prairie Pack Party 48
Wolves in the Woods 53
Alashiya and Taevas Give Gifts 55
A Very Fracture Holiday 60
A Snowy Goodeland 65
Back home in the Holler 71
Man on the Mountain 76
Sisters Celebrate 80
Fairylight 24hr Books 83
Pixie Feeding Fortunes 88
Werewolves Have a Howling Good Time 95
The Amauri-Bowan Affair 100
Divya's Gift 108
The Holiday Black Market 113
Sweet Treats for Sweet Treats 116
Tank's Worst Gift Ever 122
A Cold Diamond 127
Frozen Worlds 131
The Orclind's Biggest Party 133
Sugar and Snow 136
The Darkest Night: Sugar and Snow 2 143
The Brightest Lights: Sugar and Snow 3 152
Light the Way: Sugar and Snow 4 160
Splintered Vigil: Chapter One 171

Coming February 10th... 183
Also by Abigail Kelly 185
Glossary 187
About the Author 199
Content warnings 201

A Guide to Burden's Moon

Burden's Moon is the main winter holiday of the New Protectorate universe. It celebrates the sacrifices of the god Burden, who is tasked with carrying the world on his shoulders. Traditionally, in the Northern Hemisphere it began on the winter solstice and ended on the following full moon, but in the modern era it begins on December 21st and ends on January 21st. The first and last days are marked with feasts and are known as Moonrise and Moonset.

Moonrise is considered the family holiday, where clans and loved ones gather for an intimate meal around a fire. Gifts can be exchanged but aren't required. Moonset is the community holiday and is often celebrated with potlucks, block parties, and festivals. The time between Moonrise and Moonset is dedicated to rest, community service, and gratitude.

The monthlong holiday is rooted in community survival. When the world is at its darkest and coldest, lives depend on collective harmony, fair distribution of resources, and gathering around sources of warmth. At its heart, it's a time for family — those made and those found.

Ruffled Feathers Cafe

The holiday season hit Ruffled Feathers Cafe like an m-storm.

It was the same every year, but somehow Cassandra seemed to selectively forget all the negative aspects of it immediately after the fact. She imagined it was a bit like childbirth that way, though she'd never done that, so she couldn't say for certain.

Either way, she cursed her flock to Grim's riverbank and back when they began screaming at the unholy hour of four-thirty. It was December first, and that meant no one was safe at any time.

Wiping the sleep from her eyes, she rolled out of her nest. She free-fell toward the floor for a moment before instinct caught her. Her wings spread, catching the warm updraft, and softened her landing. Taloned feet hit the floor with a thud just as her sisters began dropping from their own nests around her.

The sound of ruffling feathers, scritching talons, and drowsy yawns were a chorus around her as she blearily sought out her dresser.

"I don't get why we do this every year. This isn't even our holiday," Lucy grumbled as she passed behind Cassandra.

"Are you really whining already?" Eugenia called out, sickeningly chipper for the hour. "That's got to be a record."

"Shut *up,*" Lucy squawked. "Not all of us wanna be a kiss-ass before sunrise."

Eugenia waited for their sister to begin to lower herself onto her vanity's stool before she kicked out with one taloned foot, knocking it out from under her. Lucy fell onto her backside with a screech, wings ruffling to a comical degree, as Eugenia threw her head back and laughed.

"Want me to kiss your ass to make it better?" she teased, hopping out of the way of Lucy's furious swipe.

Cassandra blinked hard, too tired to fall on either end of the spectrum of grumpiness just yet. Her brain didn't work properly until at *least* two cups of espresso were ingested.

As her sisters squawked and screeched, she donned a slim pair of black pants and a long-sleeved shirt. Her hair, bone-white with a smattering of chocolate brown spots and streaks, went up into a haphazard bun. Normally she put a little more sparkle into her outfit, but it was far, far too early for more effort.

While her sisters descended into a feather-pulling match, Cassandra shuffled out into the hall. The flock lived in what was once a large warehouse. It'd been converted to an aviary after the war because no one loved rafters like a flock of harpies. It took some creative engineering to separate rooms, but they'd managed to fit three families into the warehouse and still give everyone some semblance of privacy.

Well, as long as you weren't the three Colomen sisters. They'd shared a room since they were born. They'd luckily had their own nests since puberty, when Lucy and Eugenia started pushing each other out whenever they argued, but that was as far as their independence went.

Until now. Or soon, anyway.

After a quick trip to the bathroom, Cassandra meandered into the communal kitchen, where her parents and several members of the other two families — all Colomens to some degree — who made up their flock were already gathered around a box of day-old pastries.

Plastic bins of holiday decorations were neatly lined up next to the door, ready to be hauled out to the cafe. Wondering what job she'd get stuck with this year, she hurried over to the table to snag one of the good pastries before her sisters got there.

One had to be quick with food in a flock. There was no mercy amongst harpies when it came to the best bits — bloody or sugary.

Shoving half a chocolate chip muffin into her mouth, she halfheartedly greeted her aunts, uncles, and cousins as she made her way over to her mother, the ringmaster of the affair.

Standing at a towering six feet tall, with iridescent steel-gray hair and wings, Melissa Colomen was an intimidating sight even in her crescent moon-covered holiday sweater and matching barrettes. Her luminous gold eyes were fixed on the tablet in her hand, but that didn't stop her from immediately recognizing when one of her chicks was near.

Before Cassandra could so much as mutter a chocolate muffin-y hello, she was yanked into her mother's side and covered with one gray wing. "Good morning, chickadee," Melissa trilled, one hand already smoothing down the feathers of Cassandra's wings.

"Morning, Mama," she replied.

From somewhere outside the kitchen, her sisters began to shriek at one another, probably over one of them being locked out of the bathroom. Or maybe over a stolen belt. Or even just a funny look. It never took much to get them going.

"They're off to an early start," her father muttered as he walked into the room. As usual, his dark hair was meticulously combed and every shiny feather laid down with care.

Like all male harpies, he went to great lengths to impress his mate even after several decades together. It didn't matter that her mother looked at him like he hung the moon whether his feathers were groomed or not. Showing off for one's mate was simply the done thing.

Her father's wings lifted in a familiar preening stance as he neared his mate. Her mother, who looked up the moment he entered the room, met him with a whistling note.

"Good morning, my love," he said, pressing a kiss to her lips. "And good morning to my middlest chick. Are you prepared for the battle to come?"

Cassandra wrinkled her nose. "I'm not detangling the twinkle lights this year. I'm *not.* Three years in a row is cruel and unusual punishment."

"Don't worry, I've got Lucy on lights this year," her mother assured her. "You're on icicle duty."

Her father took a look at Cassandra's messy bun, sighed, and reached for her. "Turn," he instructed, clicking disapprovingly.

Stuffing the last of her muffin in her mouth, she did as she was told. While her father tugged the elastic band out of her hair and began setting her to rights, her mother called out marching orders to the assembled harpies.

Eventually her sisters made it into the kitchen, mostly unscathed, only for them to immediately start clawing at each other over the last croissant. It took two cousins, their mother, and an uncle to separate them — and split the croissant — before they finally made it out of the aviary.

"You know," her father huffed, sending clouds of condensation into the crisp pre-dawn air, "you could stand to fight with your sisters more."

Cassandra hunched her wings over her shoulders. The box of decorations was heavy in her hands but she still managed to quicken her pace a bit, hoping to outrun the conversation she'd been having with her parents since she was a child.

"I don't like fighting," she mumbled.

Her father matched her pace easily. The rest of the flock streamed ahead of them, their trilling calls and loud conversation no doubt an annoyance to anyone still trying to sleep. Their wings gleamed in a variety of colors beneath the golden glow of the street lights, but no one had Cassandra's piebald pattern of soft white and chocolate brown.

Allegedly, she took after her great-grandmother, but no one could produce a photo, so she remained unconvinced she hadn't been mixed up with the twins in the hospital and declared a triplet out of convenience. After all, what were the odds that two of the three girls would have their mother's coloring but she'd get something completely different?

It didn't matter how many times fellow harpies admired her feathers, telling her they were a good omen or that they were particularly eye-catching — the highest form of compliment for an appearance-obsessed people. Cassandra never felt like she was completely in step with her family.

It didn't help that she appeared to have been born without the desire to fight. To most harpies, her aversion to conflict was downright unnatural.

"Maybe if you just tried a little harder," her father cajoled, his face barely visible behind the stack of bins he carried. "It's good for you, chickadee. Fighting with your flock helps prepare you for the world."

"I'm plenty prepared. I've got a degree and everything." They hadn't been the most supportive of that endeavor, either, but it still meant something to her.

"But you barely leave the nest," he continued. "Your mother and I are worried that—"

"Dad, I'm doing fine. Not every harpy needs to—"

"You won't find a mate this way. How will they know you're interested if you don't fight them? And then what?"

"Not every mate needs to be bloodied to know they're being flirted with," she insisted.

No matter how many times they'd had the conversation, it never got any better. A spiky cord of anxiety wrapped around her chest and squeezed with every word out of her father's mouth.

The sight of Ruffled Feathers, their flock's communally owned cafe, up ahead was a sweet relief. Someone had already gotten inside and started turning lights on. If she hurried up, she could make it inside before her father said something inadvertently hurtful.

Well, *more* hurtful.

She quickened her steps, but it was no use. Her father, with all the love and good intentions in his heart, relentlessly continued, "No harpy worth their salt will take a mate who doesn't put up *some* fight. And if you can't find a mate, you won't have a nest of your own. You need a mate to look after you. What'll happen when your mother and I die, chickadee?"

"I'm moving out," she blurted, just inside the doorway of the cafe.

Everyone and everything stopped.

The blood drained from her cold cheeks as the flock turned to look at her with wide eyes, stunned to silence by her admission.

Her mother, who was already behind the counter preparing coffee for everyone, stared at her like she'd lost her mind. Placing her clawed hands on the glass counter, she exclaimed, "I'm sorry, *what* was that, Cass?"

Fuck.

Cassandra looked around in a panic. She hadn't intended on telling them so soon. A part of her, the cowardly part that her father couldn't resist picking at, had even considered just packing up one day and moving out while everyone was gone. They couldn't be mad if it was already done.

But *that* plan was obviously scrapped.

Giving her sisters a *please help me* look, she croaked, "Um, so, yeah... I found a place I can afford on my own. It's not far from here. I thought it'd be good to, you know, um, be more independent. Since you and Dad are always telling me that I'm too shy?"

Her sisters, for all their many annoyances, jumped to her defense as soon as her rambling petered off.

Lucy set her bin down on a table with a loud *thwump.* "I saw it! It's a great studio with a balcony and everything. Mama, you'll love it."

Eugenia, mirroring her twin, nodded enthusiastically. "And

it's so close! Just ten minutes from here. She wouldn't even have to fly to get to work on time."

"But she *could,*" Lucy interjected with a swift elbow to her sister's ribs. "You know, because of the *balcony.*"

There was a taut moment of silence as everyone waited for her mother's response. Cassandra swallowed hard, not daring to look at either of her parents. Her fingers grew sweaty from their tight grip on the edges of the plastic bin, but she worried that moving even an inch to set it down would break the fragile tension in the air.

At last, when it felt like her head was going to explode from lack of oxygen, her mother clapped her hands together and cried, "Ah, my chick is growing up!"

Taking their cue from her joyful exclamation, the rest of the flock exploded into well wishes and questions. Hands rained down on her back and playfully plucked at her feathers as she was pulled into the cafe. Someone took her bin, and within moments her father had swooped down on her to press kisses to her cheeks.

"Why didn't you say something, chickadee?" he demanded, flapping his great dark wings in proud sweeping movements.

"Um..." She ducked her head, unsure how to tell them that she had no idea if they'd approve or not.

The flock had always loved her, but they'd also looked at her like an oddball unfit for the dangers of the world. Without their aggression, she was never seen as completely grown despite the fact that she was nearing fifty years old.

"My chick gets the first latte!" her mother crowed. Swinging a clawed finger in the direction of Lucy and Eugenia, she ordered, "You two, start detangling those lights!"

Her sisters squawked with outrage before they set about their task without further argument. The cafe became a hive of warmth and activity around Cassandra as her flock filled the display cases with seasonal treats, her mother pulled perfect espresso, and her father cracked open bins full of sparkling treasures.

"Here," her mother said, placing a warm, fragrant latte in her hand. A cinnamon heart floated on the foam. Dropping a kiss onto the crown of Cassandra's head, she murmured, "I hope you know we're going to be over all the time. There's no escaping the flock, chickadee."

Clutching the cup to her chest, Cassandra let out a relieved breath. "Promise?"

"Promise." Her mother's wing swept behind her back, urging Cassandra toward her father. "Now get decorating! We open in an hour!"

Solbourne Feast

DECEMBER 2043 — SAN FRANCISCO, THE ELVISH PROTECTORATE

Theodore couldn't remember a time when Burden's Moon wasn't a grand affair in Solbourne Tower, and for that he would always be grateful.

His mother had apparently started the tradition of transforming the Tower for the holiday. Despite the fact that he had no memories of the woman who'd died to protect him, he felt a little closer to her when the lights and crystal moons were hung in the gleaming lobby.

Although elves primarily worshipped Glory, Burden had a special place in their hearts. The god of home, hearth, clan, and responsibility, he was the consort to their beloved goddess. The world rested on his shoulders, and if he hadn't reached into the Earth to present his mate with a gift of jewels, elves wouldn't exist.

And elves did nothing halfway, including celebrations.

Theodore passed beneath the massive chandelier hung above the lobby. He cast it an admiring look as he made his way to the bank of elevators that would take him home.

Made of hundreds of pine boughs, lit by artificial candles, and dripping with real crystal icicles and moons in different phases, it was a perfect centerpiece for the opulently decorated heart of the Tower.

"Andy's outdone herself this year," he noted, nudging Kaz.

His brother looked up with a grunt. "That's a hazard. What if there's an earthquake?"

"Not everything is a safety risk," he shot back, nodding to the elves who stepped out of his way. Even at the start of the holiday, the lobby was packed with jewel-toned people, and all of them watched him with varying degrees of reverence or hostility. "Some things are just pretty, Kaz. Lighten up."

His brother hit the up button on the elevator's panel without looking away from the phone in his hand. "You work with my people long enough and you'll reevaluate that stance," he muttered.

The metal doors slid open. Theodore stepped inside with a barely audible sigh, the muscles between his shoulder blades relaxing a bit. There were many things he loved about being the first in line to take over the territory, but the constant scrutiny wasn't one of them. Never, not once, did he get to truly breathe easy when he was out among the public.

The future sovereign didn't get to be normal. He didn't get to be unobserved. He didn't get to show weakness or reveal how tired he was.

Especially when no one wanted him to take the job.

But when he stepped into the family's private elevator, his brother by his side, he wasn't just the sovereign-in-waiting. He was Teddy, and Teddy got to breathe.

Leaning against the elevator's wall, he unsnapped the silver thistle pin that kept his starched collar in place. It was on the tip of his tongue to ask Kaz about his team of feral assassins, but Theodore smothered the impulse. It was a holiday. He'd spent too much of it working already. For one night, he wanted to just... be.

"Is Sam in yet?" he asked instead.

"Landed an hour ago," Kaz replied, pocketing his phone. He

tucked his big green hands into his beaten leather jacket and matched Theodore's pose on the opposite wall. "So you know Winnie has him setting the table or something already."

Theodore cracked a smile, but it was brief. "How long is he staying?"

Kaz shook his head. "Not long enough. A week, I think."

Disappointment soured his stomach. Running his tongue along his upper fangs, Theodore tried to tamp down the impulse to complain.

Samuel had valid reasons for not wanting to stay in the city for even a moment longer than he had to, but that didn't mean it hurt less every time he escaped to his compound in the desert.

Looking at his brother out of the corner of his eye, he asked, "You're sticking around, right?"

Kaz shrugged. "Sue called and asked if I'd spend some time on the ranch, but I told her no."

"She could come here," he offered, as he always did. "Your family's always welcome. I would love to—"

"Teddy," Kaz gruffly interjected, "I know. But you can't fix this for me, no matter how much you want to. Frances would never let Sue step foot in elvish territory, let alone come *here.*"

It wasn't like Theodore could blame Kaz's grandmother for her hesitation — or outright hatred — but it went against something fundamental in him to just sit back and do nothing. He didn't work as hard as he did because of some inherent love of responsibility or patriotism. He did it for the people he loved.

But what good did any of it do if his brother couldn't embrace both sides of his family? Or if Samuel couldn't bear to show his face in his own home? Or if Valen stayed up for days at a time, terrified of what would happen when the public learned of Delilah's abdication?

What's the point if I can never find her?

A sharp pain slid between his ribs as he reached out through the haze of great distance toward the beacon of light and warmth that was his consort.

Was she well? Was she surrounded by loving family, warm and safe during the darkest night of the year? It drove him mad to not know.

Theodore stared at his warped reflection in the elevator's doors. They were slowing to a stop after the long, smooth climb toward the penthouse, but he felt like he'd left his stomach somewhere on the ground floor.

A heavy hand landed on his shoulder and squeezed. He looked up at his brother just as the elevator doors began to open.

"Hey," Kaz rumbled, giving his shoulder a hearty shake. "Let it go. It's a holiday. You've been working yourself to death. Just enjoy the night, huh?"

Theodore looked into the hard lines of his brother's striking face. Sometimes he wondered what it would've been like if his mother lived, or if his father never met Amira. In a perfect world, his bastard father would've gotten his head on straight after he met his consort and abandoned life in elvish society. Then they could've had it all: his mother alive, his brother unscarred, and Kaz still in their lives.

But it hadn't worked out like that, and he wasn't selfish enough to be ungrateful for the gifts he'd been given.

"Yeah," he replied, summoning a smile. He clapped his brother on the shoulder with a playful growl. "C'mon. I'm hungry."

They stepped out into the warded hallway. One never truly got used to the oppressive, sinister air of that protective barrier, but they had a lot of practice ignoring it. The men chatted amiably as they passed under the bloody sigils and into the much more hospitable main atrium of the family's quarters.

Kaz let out a low whistle as he beheld the towering silver moon that had been erected in the center of the floor. It was surrounded by what looked like every pillar candle in the city, as well as bouquets of seasonal flowers. Garlands dripped from the massive glass dome over their heads, scenting the room with spicy pine.

Across the atrium, the door to the family's main living quarters opened with a bang. Golden light spilled out across the floor, silhouetting Winnie.

"Boys!" she called out, her gorgeous face split with a grin. "Come on! Your brother brought a board game he says is Foresight and psychic-proof. We have to start soon so your grandfather can't beg off with an excuse about an old man needing his beauty sleep again."

Theodore tossed his head back with a dramatic sigh but he didn't stop walking toward the woman who was, in all the ways that mattered, his mother. "Can't I change into something comfortable first?"

He and Kaz bent down to press the required kisses to her deep ruby cheeks. Winnie kissed them both in turn, as if it'd been weeks since she saw them last and not a day at most. "If you had been on *time,* you could've changed," she admonished him before delivering one final smacking kiss to his other cheek.

"Negotiations ran long," he sheepishly explained.

Fixing the collar of Kaz's leather jacket, she demanded, "And what's your excuse?"

"Vesta stabbed Arjun over control of the remote." Kaz sent Theodore a pointed look. "I *told* you giving them free access to television was a bad idea."

Winnie, long used to Fracture's ways, simply rolled her eyes. "Well, you're here, so I can assume no one died."

"Not yet," he sighed.

"Come on, come on." She ushered them inside. Both men, fully grown and nearly twice her size, followed obediently after her as she led them down the hall decorated in dozens of Delilah's paintings.

When they reached the lavish family sitting room, they were met with even more glittering decorations, a roaring fire, and nearly all the people he loved. A low table had been set up where the usual coffee table normally sat, and it'd been covered in a white table cloth embroidered with silver moons. Silver platters of raw meat, some seasoned and some left plain, were scattered across it. Green candles in faceted crystal holders flickered between them and made the blood glitter.

Andy hovered by the overflowing drink cart, clearly whipping up a new holiday beverage that would get them all slammed well before any of them suspected, while Valen sat spread-legged on a leather armchair, looking sleepy-eyed and at ease for once.

Samuel stood with his back to the fire, a drink already in his hand, with his head bent toward Delilah. They seemed to be having some sort of intense conversation, but he knew it was useless to wonder what it was about. They wouldn't explain even if he asked.

Those two shared a special bond that only two beings capable of Foresight could. If it brought them a little bit of peace to share some things only with each other, then he couldn't fault them for it.

Mostly.

"At last, the wayward boys have arrived," Winnie announced with a flourish.

Valen raised his glass with a grandfatherly grunt while his consort looked over her shoulder and called out, "Finally! Come grab a drink. And give me a kiss, for Glory's sake."

Delilah peered at them from her place by the mantle. Standing in the shadow of their mother's portrait which hung in its gilded frame over the crackling fire, she gave them a look of uncanny confusion. "Where's Viktor?"

Theodore winced. It'd been years since Viktor joined them for any family event, but she never seemed to remember.

Giving her a gentle look, he answered, "He's not coming this year, Lilah."

"Oh." She wrinkled her nose. "That's rude. We're family."

Crossing the room to give her a kiss on the cheek, he agreed, "It's very rude. Maybe someday he'll pull his head out of his ass and join us again."

Her heavy sigh brushed his ear. "There are too many people missing. It's not the same."

The holidays — all of them — were difficult for his sister, but he thought that perhaps Burden's Moon was the hardest for her to endure. The woman who stared serenely out at them from the canvas over her shoulder loomed even larger in his sister's fragile mind, and sometimes the shadow of her loss made it harder than normal for Delilah to connect with the present.

Samuel, who understood Delilah better than any of them, draped an arm over her shoulders. "Let's break out the game, huh? We have more than enough people here for *that.*"

Brightening immediately, she took a large swig of her drink before swanning off toward the food, her melancholy forgotten almost as quickly as it arrived. "I'm going to kick *everyone's* ass," she declared, plucking a strip of cured salmon off a platter. Wiggling it in the air, she sent her consort a cheeky wink. "Except my Winnie, of course. I'll happily kiss hers."

"There are parents present!" Valen called out with a heavy roll of his eyes.

"You better let me win," Winnie sing-songed as she sashayed toward Delilah, her own drink in hand.

Pressing a loud, smacking kiss to her lips, Delilah promised, "Always, my love."

Turning away from the display with a fond shake of his head, Theodore yanked his brother into a tight hug. Samuel barely escaped it before Kaz did the same.

"Welcome home!" Theodore slapped his back once, but when Kaz followed it up with his own slap, it became a game to see who could smack him the most and quickest.

"Good gods, you monsters need to leave me alone," Samuel grunted, swatting at them with his pale, ungloved claws.

"But we *missed* you," Kaz drawled, smacking him even harder.

Theodore, seeing his brother had bigger hands and therefore more impactful slaps, switched to grabbing Samuel by the biceps and giving him a good, brotherly shake. "So much! Didn't you miss us? Huh?"

"For fuck's sake..." Samuel sighed, and in one blindingly fast movement managed to not only slip from Theodore's hold, but snag them *both* around their necks in shockingly efficient chokeholds.

"Must we *every* time I come home? Really?"

He gave them both a hard squeeze. Despite the fact that Samuel appeared quite a bit leaner than his brothers, he was by all accounts a superior fighter. That probably had something to do with the fact that he could predict exactly what his opponents were going to do the second before they chose to do it, but it was also because of the horrifying expectations their father had laid on his perfect heir — before Kaz was born, anyway.

"You're menaces," he said, still using that soft, raspy voice that never seemed to hold any anger or urgency. "Who raised you, anyway?"

"Hey!" Winnie gave them all the stink eye. Pointing one diamond-tipped claw at them, she ordered, "No sparring and no blackouts until *after* we play a game. Understood?"

Always quick to do whatever Winnie said, Samuel immediately answered, "Yes, ma'am."

He nearly released them, too, but Kaz choked out, "Suck-up."

Throwing Theodore away from him, Samuel put the full force of his body weight into turning Kaz's much denser frame toward the fire. "What was that? You want to see how flammable you are? You know, I've always wondered."

Howling with laughter, Theodore stumbled backward and nearly smashed into the table. Their dinner was saved by Andy, who caught him by the scruff of his collar. Smiling, she gave him a good shake. "You started this. What kind of behavior is that for a future sovereign?"

"I didn't do anything!" he complained, struggling to hide his laughter as his brothers twisted and contorted themselves in an attempt to force each other into the fire. It wouldn't hurt them, but it *would* annoy Winnie to have to break out the fire extinguisher so early in the evening.

"Kaz, *twist* your hips! Use your momentum, for pity's sake," Valen called out. "You have a weight advantage!"

Winnie threw her hands up in the air when Delilah cheered for Samuel. "Do not encourage— Samuel Thaddeus Solbourne, if you stick your brother's head in the fire I am going to throw your gifts in with him!"

Shucking his suit jacket and carelessly tossing it onto the floor, Theodore rolled up his sleeves, clapped his gloved hands together, and ran headlong back into the fray. A roar of laughter exploded from Kaz as they took on their older brother in an objectively unfair fight.

At some point, it stopped being about trying to throw someone in the fire and turned to simply pinning the wily red-haired sibling to the ground. While Delilah called out pointers and Valen criticized their moves, Andy and Winnie retreated to the couch, resigned to wait out their annual wrestling match.

Laughter erupted as they grappled, using every dirty trick in the book, and the golden light of the fire winked in the glasses their audience brought to their lips. All the while, their mother's portrait watched over them, a soft smile on her lips, and the white-hot glow of his consort burned in Theodore's mind, reminding him that no one was ever really gone.

They were with him every step of the way.

Wilson Family Dinner

It was an odd thing, welcoming someone new into a clan. He'd thought so way back when Seamus was born and again with every subsequent sibling's entrance, but he figured it'd get a little less awkward now that everyone involved was grown.

I guess even I can be wrong sometimes, he thought.

Harrison leaned back in the armchair he'd claimed, a beer in hand, as he observed his littlest brother and his new mate setting out the good plates for their Moonrise dinner. He didn't mean to stare, but he couldn't help it.

Nelly was an odd bird.

He'd been away from Montague for years now, but he had no trouble imagining what the tiny town's reception to the witch must've been. She looked hilariously out of place standing next to his grinning little brother — who, for reasons he'd yet to work out, wore a floral button down.

Knee-high to a frog, decked out in a frothy ruffled dress that barely reached mid-thigh, and... *witchy,* Nelly Ortega was the single strangest thing he'd ever seen in his mama's kitchen. And that was saying something, knowing that things Clark and Penny got up to.

"I know he *said* he'd found a mate," Seamus muttered under

his breath as he dropped into the chair beside Harrison's, "but I still kinda thought it was a prank."

Harrison sniffed. "Still kinda feels like a prank. A witch in a clan of orcs? C'mon."

Seamus, a barrel-chested, green-skinned orc who made his living with his hands, rolled his massive shoulders back with a heavy sigh. "See, I thought the joke was that he met somebody before us. I mean, what're the odds? And that *story.* Ran his truck into a tree only to wake up bonded *and* have the kohl? All without having to leave the comfort of his hometown. Fucker didn't even have to try."

He couldn't blame Seamus for his disbelief. The story was fantastical — like the convoluted plot to one of those cheesy films he did his best to avoid.

But the proof was in the kohl, as they said. There was no denying the dark tint to Clark's hands, which he'd proudly showed off to both his brothers the second they swung into town. A mate was a mate, and their little brother was damn pleased with the one the gods had given him.

"Well, if some bullshit like that was gonna happen, it'd happen to Clark," Harrison replied, lips quirking in a smile. "I guess it figures he'd end up with someone so..."

Not needing him to finish the sentence, Seamus nodded emphatically. "A-yup."

A squeal of laughter from the dining room drew their gazes to Penny, who Clark had hoisted up by her underarms. "I'm not a baby!" she cried, cackling madly. "You can't put me at the kid's table anymore!"

"You're barely old enough to drink," Clark replied.

"So? How dare you—"

"And you're my baby sister for all eternity. *And* you just tried to take my spot next to *my* mate, so you're officially banished to the kid's table!"

Nelly, who casually continued to place silverware around the table with her gloved hands, calmly interjected, "Penny, I don't have any brothers, so I don't know if this is normal behavior. Please blink twice if you need me to intervene. I can also deliver retribution on your behalf later. Just give me the signal. I know where he sleeps."

"Sugar!" Clark exclaimed, giving his mate his patented puppy dog eyes. Setting his still giggling sister aside, he asked, "How could you—"

Arching her brows, she gave her mate a look Harrison had seen his mother aim his father's way many, many times. *"Easily."*

"But I thought you loved—"

Wiggling a shiny spoon in front of her mate's nose, she drawled, "How quickly you forget eating the last cinnamon roll, Mr. Ortega. Would that I could forget just as easily!"

Seamus let loose a whistle. "Taking food outta your own mate's mouth? Damn, boy, I thought we brought you up better." Leaning forward in his seat with a big, shit-eating grin that showed off his large lower fangs, he added, "Wanna switch Wilsons, Nelly? I'd never betray you that way."

Clark threw up his hands. "Hey! Stop trying to steal my mate!"

"As much as it pains me, I think I'm stuck with the one I've got." Nelly finished setting the silverware down and sidled up beside Clark, who slung a muscular arm over her thin shoulders without a second of hesitation. In a coordinated movement that appeared seamless, she tilted her head back as he stooped. They shared a smiling kiss, like they were passing a secret between them — or perhaps like they'd already shared all their secrets.

Harrison wasn't all that comfortable welcoming strangers into the clan, but *that*... Yeah, he could see the appeal of something like that.

Pineridge Potluck

Antonia wasn't entirely certain how she'd been roped into organizing Pineridge's annual Moonset potluck, but it was definitely her sister's fault.

She liked to think that as an experienced healer, she wasn't easy to ruffle. After all, she'd cut her teeth in the emergency ward of the largest hospital in the Shifter Alliance. Hardly a moment went by without some life-or-death emergency she was required to handle promptly and with the stoic professionalism her kind were known for.

Compared to bloody forty-eight hour shifts and sedated wolves trying to take a bite out of her backside, her new practice in Pineridge was comically easy.

Or it *was* until her sister volunteered them for potluck duty.

"How many times do I have to say I'm sorry before you forgive me? You know how I get flustered when people start asking me for things! And I forgot I promised to bring Isabel to her dad's parents' this year. I swear it wasn't intentional," Dara sighed. She had to speak loudly into the phone's speaker to be heard over the music of her daughter's favorite new boy band.

Grimacing at the yellowed piece of paper in her hand,

Antonia replied, "I don't know. How many people are in this phone tree? Let me count."

"Phone tree? What is this, this 1950's? Has no one in Pineridge heard of a groupchat?"

Getting up to make herself something hot to drink, she snarked, "Maybe you should ask the town council — you know, since you're such good friends with them."

"Annie, this is a great opportunity for you," Dara needled. "You want to get to know the community, the community wants to get to know you..."

She snorted as she set the kettle on the cooker. "Wow, thank you for the amazing opportunity."

Ignoring her sister's sarcastic tone, Dara replied, "You're *so* welcome. Okay, we're pulling up now. Good luck!"

"Dara—"

Antonia pulled the phone away from her ear with a groan. Watching the steam begin to rise from the kettle's spout, she drummed her nails on the counter and tried to think of a plan.

"It's just a potluck," she muttered. "I've done surgery before. How hard can it be?"

Two weeks and approximately a hundred phone calls later, Antonia discovered that organizing a community potluck could, in fact, be harder than surgery.

Paloma, her heavily pregnant patient and neighbor, stood beside her at the long, plastic-covered table. Holding her hands to the small of her back, she noted, "Well, at least we didn't get *all* cookies. Look, there's mac and cheese! And Laura brought biscuits."

Antonia stared at the sad spread with resignation. "It's all desserts," she muttered, dumbfounded. "I don't know what happened, Paloma."

"Well, what'd you tell people to bring?"

"I... said to bring a dish," she answered, counting the trays of sweets again, just in case she'd hallucinated the first time.

Paloma made a knowing sound. "Is that *all* you said?"

Glancing at her patient who'd quickly become a friend, she replied, "Yes? Why?"

"Ah." Paloma laid a hand on her shoulder and gave it a good, pitying pat. "You made a rookie mistake. See, if you don't tell people explicitly that they need to bring an entree, everyone chooses store-bought dessert. It's potluck 101, Antonia."

"What? Since *when—*"

"Where's all the meat?" A playful, lightly accented voice came from behind her.

By the time Antonia had turned to see Artem, the dragon had already swooped in on his mate. His long tail wrapped around Paloma's heavy belly with a possessive stroke as he leaned down to press a kiss to the top of her head.

"You're early!" Paloma exclaimed, half-turning to grin up at her mate. "I thought your meeting—"

Artem, dressed in a fine suit of navy velvet with gold trim, stroked his mate's cheek with the back of a claw. "Not even elves can say no to wrapping up early when I explain I have a pregnant mate waiting for me," he rumbled.

"That's nice," Antonia butted in, "but did you happen to bring an entree with you?"

Artem glanced between her and Paloma, his horned brow furrowed with confusion. "No, Healer Belton. My mate said she was bringing brownies."

Throwing up her hands, Antonia groaned, *"Everyone* brought brownies! Or cookies! Or *lemon bars!"*

The hair rose on the back of her neck a moment before a low, amused voice murmured in her ear, "Then it's a good thing I decided on ham, then."

A full-body flush rolled through her, entirely involuntary and unwanted, as she whirled around to find a golden-haired shifter hovering behind her.

Jack gave her a slow smile. Dressed in a leather jacket with his hair perfectly wind-swept, he carried a massive covered platter in his gloved hands.

Her heart leapt, and if she pretended it was because he'd probably rescued the potluck, then that was fine.

"You brought ham?" she gasped, already reaching for the platter.

Jack swung it up and out of her reach effortlessly, showing off that notorious shifter strength. "Careful, Healer. It's hot!"

"Well, put it on the table," she ordered, already turning to move the many plates of sweets out of the way. "Come on, before anyone sees!"

Laughing, the shifter leaned around her — a little too close — to set the platter down with a theatrical flourish. "What happened?" he teased. "You didn't let everyone decide for themselves what they'd bring, did you?"

Exasperated, she hissed, "How was I supposed to know everyone would bring sweets?"

"Coulda asked me for help," he whispered, that charming half-smile still on his lips.

Antonia sniffed. "Really? Because last time I checked, you don't answer my calls."

His smile dimmed, but Jack was no less handsome when he was serious. In her experience, shifters were always magnetic. It had something to do with the raw energy they possessed. Even when they were the worst people you'd ever met, they were hard to look away from.

And Jack was hardly the worst person she'd ever met. He just happened to be entirely full of himself.

"That's business," he argued. "Now, if you want to talk about personal things..."

"A potluck isn't *personal.*"

"It is if everyone talks about how it became a bake sale for the rest of the year," he laughed.

"It's her first time organizing a potluck," Paloma interjected, laughter in her voice. "Cut her some slack."

Straightening, Jack raised a hand in greeting. "Hey Polly." His tone lost most of its warmth when he turned his attention to

Artem, who watched him with a narrowed-eyed look of cool hostility. "Aždaja."

"Jack Jr," the dragon drawled. One huge, leathery wing curved over his mate's shoulder to drape over her belly.

Antonia watched the interaction with interest for all of a second before aiming her attention where it belonged: reorganizing the buffet table so it looked like there was an actual dinner to be had.

There was bad blood between those two, but not the kind she had any professional or personal investment in. So Antonia artfully arranged her edamame salad next to Jack's offering and ignored the sounds of Paloma making a hurried excuse to put distance between the two men.

"The hall looks nice," Jack noted. He leaned his hip against the table and crossed his arms.

Antonia looked around briefly, taking in the silver garlands and large, iridescent moons hung from string that dangled from scotch tape stuck to the ceiling. She'd done her best with the decorations she'd found in the community center's storage, but no one had ever said she had an eye for that sort of thing.

"Thanks," she muttered, pulling the lid off the platter.

"Where's your sister and Isabel?"

Antonia slid him a look out of the corner of her eye. "Where's your father?"

Jack's lips pressed thin. "With the pack."

Shocker.

The Grand Sierra pack wasn't the most social group she'd ever met, and Jack Sr. was even more reclusive. According to Paloma, he hadn't been a big fan of the previous healer, and it appeared that had been transferred over to her. The only member who had any interest in her or her clinic was Jack Jr., and she was fairly certain *that* had nothing to do with her services.

In her experience, most shifters were incorrigible flirts. She didn't take Jack's advances any more seriously than she had from all the shifters who came before him. Or she tried not to, anyway. It was admittedly a *little* more difficult than normal.

"Well, you'll have to take some cookies home for him," she replied, handing Jack a paper plate. Just when his fingers curled around the edge, she yanked it back toward her. Leaning in close, she casually offered, "Or I could take them myself and save you the trouble. While I'm there I could give him that check-up he's been dodging."

Bending at the waist, Jack whispered, "You don't need an excuse to come by our territory, dream girl. I'll give you a tour."

Smiling, she released the plate. "Oh, I know. Your cousin Joshua offered to take me around last week. I'll just give him a call, hm?"

Liquid gold flashed in his hazel eyes, but Jack's easy expression didn't falter. "Joshua, huh? Interesting."

"Is it?" she asked breezily. Plopping a store bought sugar cookie shaped to look like a crescent moon onto his plate, she gave him what she hoped was a convincingly nonchalant smile. "Enjoy the potluck, mountain lion."

Jack brought the cookie to his lips. "With you here? It'd be impossible not to."

Knowing she had to get away from him quickly to escape the gravitational pull of shifter magnetism, she hurried toward where townspeople clad in fluffy winter coats were streaming through the doors.

Still, she was incapable of letting him have the last word.

Calling over her shoulder, she said, "Oh, and Jack?"

There was a husky note in his voice that made her stomach swoop when he replied, "Yeah, dream girl?"

"Try the salad."

Empire Estate Celebrates

Syndicate life wasn't all about death and law-breaking. To make the darkness worth it, there had to be moments of profound release.

And that meant the men of Empire Estate's security team knew how to party.

Unfortunately.

Michael let out a low groan. A hangover throbbed behind his eyes as he squinted at the communal guard quarters, where the security team's party had been held. With Zia and Harlan away visiting her family overseas for the holiday, most of the security team had been left to their own devices.

It was a mistake.

Praying his pain pill would kick in soon, Michael kicked aside alcoholic synth bottles strewn across the floor. Despite the fact that demons had impeccable night vision, he squinted at the shapes scattered around the room. He was pretty sure they were men, but in the state they were all in, one couldn't be sure.

The blackout blinds had come down automatically, shielding the vampires from the blinding sunlight bouncing off the snow outside. That was good, because not a single one of them had been sober enough to remember to pull them down before they passed out.

If Atticus had been there, he would've remembered. He was the responsible one. But he and his little sister had gone with Harlan and Zia, which meant he'd deputized Michael as The One In Charge.

And that was why he was up while the rest of them were slobbering on couch pillows or laying face down beneath the pool table. He would've loved to join them — after emptying both his stomach and his bladder — but he could not, *would not* let Atticus come back to find vomit on the floor, Damien's knife collection embedded in various walls, and Archie's bare gargoyle ass stuck in the air.

Why Archie was nude, Michael couldn't rightly recall. He'd lost track of things sometime around his third bottle of tequila and fifth catastrophic loss in poker. If he had to guess, it had something to do with demonstrating traditional highland gargoyle combat techniques, but he had no intention of asking.

Shuffling stiffly toward where he vaguely recalled the light switch to be, Michael closed his eyes and braced himself.

Don't throw up, he silently coached himself. *You'll have to clean it. Don't throw up. Don't throw up...*

Girding himself, he skimmed his hand along the smooth plaster wall until he found the switch. After a moment of hesitation, he flipped on the light.

"Turn off the fucking *light!"* Damien yowled.

Shoving his face into the couch cushions, the normally collected vampire curled into himself like a sad little shrimp. When he put on silk pajamas and why, Michael really couldn't say. He was pretty sure they didn't actually belong to Damien, though.

Eyes watering with the glare, Michael rasped, "We've got an hour until sunset. Two hours until the boss is back. We have to get our shit right or Atticus is gonna beat our asses."

"You just wanna impress Adriana," Archie muttered, Scottish

accent thicker than normal, from his sprawled pose on the bean bag chair. His nearly indestructible wings came up to cover his head, shielding him from the light. "Look at this demon. He's *so* clean. So *responsible.* Michael and Adriana sitting in a—"

The back of his neck heated with a vengeance. It was a deeply unfortunate truth that at one point early on in his employment, he'd had a very small, very brief crush on Atticus's beautiful little sister. It died a quick death when he realized that Adriana had no interest in him and that Atticus would, with zero hesitation, cut off both his hands if he ever tried to make a move.

Unfortunately, he wasn't exactly skilled at being subtle, and his fumbling attempts to flirt had been witnessed by the other men. Despite the fact that it'd been a decade since he had feelings for her, they liked to bring it up at every opportunity.

The only way to get them to shut up, he discovered, was violence.

Michael picked up the nearest empty tequila bottle from the floor and chucked it at the gargoyle's bare ass. It exploded into a shower of glass with a tremendous noise that made every hung over man in the room cry out.

Stomping over to the pool table, he grabbed Tarrance by the ankle and yanked him out from beneath it. "Up," he grunted, releasing the whining shifter with a light kick to his side.

A chorus of complaints arose from around the room, but they cut off abruptly when he growled, "If you don't care about Atticus seeing your vomit on the carpet, then think about Zia. You want *her* to see your ass, Archie?"

The gargoyle's wings tensed. In a smaller voice, he replied, "No."

"No's right, because the boss would skin you alive."

"She said she was bringing gifts," Damien mumbled into the cushions. "She said that, right?"

Several muttered affirmatives went around the room. Michael eyed the vampire hanging over the loft's bannister when he ordered, "Come on, boys. We can't let our girl see us like this."

"All right, all right," Tarrance wheezed as he climbed onto his hands and knees. Swiping a half-full bottle of vodka from the floor, he raised it into the air and proclaimed, "For our girl! And Burden, I guess."

Snatching the bottle out of his hand just before it touched his lips, Michael sighed, "I think we did enough celebrating."

Tarrance raised his head and squinted red-rimmed eyes at the disaster that was their communal space. Gagging a little, he replied, "You're probably right."

Princess Astrid Lights the Flame

They were fighting again. As usual, it was her fault.

Astrid knew she shouldn't listen, but that was one rule she was no good at following.

She pressed her green ear against the smooth wall of her nest and held her breath. Her father's baritone reverberated through the layers of plaster and fine, hand-hewn wood that separated her bedroom from her parents' suite.

"...coddle her, Dagur!"

She flinched away from the skin-warmed plaster. Astrid's stomach knotted as tightly as the braid that kept her long raven hair out of her face. That tone haunted her, waking and sleeping. Her mother's voice was like a knife. The cuts it left took a long time to heal, and just when they did, the blade came out again.

The worst was when Astrid knew her mother was right to be angry.

She *had* messed up. She deserved to be the one taking the cuts, not her father. But his baritone rumbled through the wall all the same.

"Has it ever occurred to you that she's a *child?* Children ought to be coddled now and then!"

"She's not a child," her mother snapped. "She's a princess of the Orclind and future matriarch of the Seagrim Clan. Good gods, I'd already killed a man by her age!"

"And look how you turned out!"

Her mother's snarl sent a chill down Astrid's spine. "I led this territory through a century of war!"

Her father never raised his voice. He didn't need to. Instead, he said things with such a calm, effortless clarity that the truth of it carried a devastating impact.

"You led this territory *into* war," he replied, "and I pray every day that our daughter has more mercy in her heart than you. The gods gifted her some softness and I thank them for it."

"Mercy? She'll be lucky to live long enough to *lead,* let alone be merciful!"

"It was a few tears, Sigrid," her father shot back. "She's *seven.* She got overwhelmed. You put a child in front of nearly a million people and told her to perform a rite that would be hard for an adult to remember. What did you expect?"

"I expected her to do her duty. That's all I ever expect of her, and yet somehow she continues to fail." There was a desperate edge in her voice when she continued, "How will she survive the court if she can't even light a fire, my mate? If she shows this much weakness—"

There was a pause. Astrid squeezed her eyes shut and bit her lip, willing the tears to stay locked inside.

She hadn't meant to mess it up. All she'd done for a week was practice the rite, and she'd been so, so looking forward to the first night of Burden's Moon. She'd never been allowed to attend the Moonrise festival before. It'd been everything she dreamed of: a sea of jubilant orcs gathered around hundreds of bonfires, fireworks bursting in the sky, the scents of smoke and rich food blending with snow in the air…

But when she climbed the steps with her mother and that unimaginably large sprawl of people went silent, Astrid couldn't do it. She didn't know why. The words just wouldn't come. With every second that passed, the worse it got.

When her mother looked down at her with that familiar disapproving glare, she'd shut down entirely. Her chance to light the flame vanished the moment the first tear escaped.

She didn't see her father sprint up the steps, but she'd been so glad when he swooped her up into his arms and shielded her from the murmuring crowd. His rumbling purr soothed her panicked sobs and the touch of his kohl-darkened hands to her elaborately styled hair was a balm to her dashed hopes.

But comfort was always fleeting. Astrid knew there'd be a reckoning when they returned to the palace. Her mother hadn't even looked at her the entire ride home. That was always a bad sign.

When even the staff wouldn't meet her gaze as they helped prepare her for bed, she knew it was very bad indeed.

Softer voices filtered through the wall — her mother's and her father's, gentled by some understanding she couldn't grasp. Astrid couldn't hear what they spoke of now, only that peculiar tone. It was something like sadness, and that was worse than anger.

She turned away from the wall.

I need to do better, she thought, dragging her comforter up to her nose to muffle the sobs she couldn't quite stop. *Why couldn't I just say the words? I know them. Papa taught me. Why was I so scared?*

Her father had assured her that stage fright was perfectly normal, but in her heart she knew it wasn't the crowd that had scared her.

It was her mother, and that shamed her.

She wasn't sure how long it took, but eventually her tears stopped flowing. Astrid stared at the silver-embroidered roof of her nest with dry, itchy eyes. Exhaustion made her small limbs heavy, but sleep refused to come.

That meant she was still awake when the door to her bedroom

opened. From beyond the heavy curtains of her nest, her father whispered, "My star, are you sleeping?"

Her heart squeezed so hard, it nearly knocked the wind out of her.

Astrid sat up and scrambled toward the entrance of the nest. Pushing the curtains aside, she answered, "Papa?"

He was barely visible in the thin sliver of warm light that spilled from the nearly closed bedroom door, but she'd know the shape of her father's broad shoulders and stocky frame anywhere.

Only the whites of his eyes and teeth were truly visible when he said, "Do you have a moment for your papa? I have a surprise for you."

Overwhelmed with the relief of having him near, she scrambled to push the curtain open for him. "Come in!"

"Thank you, my star," he rumbled.

She scooted back into the nest as he squeezed in. That was no easy feat, considering his size, but he didn't complain about the cramped conditions as he laid back onto her pillows. Astrid cuddled into his side immediately, drawn into the comforting warmth of her father's embrace.

His scent, smoke and green grass, eased the terrible knots in her belly. Nothing seemed quite so bad when her father was with her. Not even failing her mother.

"I had a feeling you wouldn't be sleeping," he sighed, hugging her close with one arm. "Were you listening to me and your mama again?"

"Yes," she admitted, unable to lie to him.

He *tsked.* "I wish you wouldn't."

"I wish you wouldn't fight so much," she replied, pressing her face into his chest.

He sounded tired when he said, "I know, my star. I know."

"I'm sorry I—"

"You did *nothing* wrong, Astrid," he cut in, voice hardening. "You're a good girl. All you ever do is your best. If your mama and

I fight, it's because we both love you too much. We can't always agree on the best way to help you, and that means we lose our heads."

"If I'd just lit the fire, you wouldn't have fought at all," she sniffed.

"Ah, well, who can say? The fun part of adulthood is that there's always something silly to fight about." Patting her back, he added, "And there's still time for you to light the flame, my star."

Astrid sat up a little. Squinting at her father's shadowed face, she asked, "How? The festival—"

"Doesn't matter. The holiday continues with or without us. That means we can have our own traditions." Pulling her back into his side, her father reached into what she could only guess was his back pocket.

"Here," he said, putting what felt suspiciously like a pack of matches in her little hand. "Light the flame, Princess Astrid."

She stared at the small white candle he held before her. Eyes watering, she warbled, "Really?"

"Go on," he encouraged.

Her hand shook so badly it took her several tries to strike the match, but when it lit, it seemed as bright as the sun in that soft, dark space. The metallic scent of the matchstrike bloomed in the air, as sharp and strange as magic.

Her breath trembled when she dutifully recited, "We gather the wood. We gather the clan. We gather the stone. We gather the children. We light the flame. We light the way. May Burden's sacrifice never go unseen, and may his love n—never— never go unfelt."

She nearly dropped the match when she tried to light the wick, but her father steadied her hand just in time. He guided it toward the candle with all the gentle confidence he did everything.

Something warm and powerful expanded in her chest as she watched the wick catch. A gentle sphere of light illuminated her father's beloved face, all hard angles and tough green skin. He held the candle carefully between them when he leaned down to press a kiss to her forehead.

"Perfect, my star," he murmured. "You're perfect, and your parents love you. Never doubt that."

Merfolk in the Moonlight

Being broken up with was never fun, but being dumped during Burden's Moon? That was a next level sort of shitty even Louisa, who knew a thing or two about raw deals, hadn't experienced before.

Huddled in the cold sand, dressed in her holiday finest, and clutching a stupidly expensive to-go cup of hot chocolate, she was a miserable wreck.

Why she thought the ocean would soothe her sorrows, she had no idea. She'd never been a nature girl. She barely knew how to swim, and large bodies of unchlorinated water had always seemed like hostile alien worlds to her.

Even if there weren't man-eating merfolk in there, she didn't understand the appeal of venturing into a place where people weren't the top dogs.

Maybe that was a failure of her imagination, or perhaps another symptom of what Greg called her "boring brain". She wasn't *fun.* She didn't like taking risks and couldn't see why others did. She didn't want to try new things when a perfectly good, familiar choice sat right in front of her.

Louisa thought her risk aversion made her a good, stable partner. Greg didn't agree.

That was how she'd ended up at the Aquatic Park, the only land-dweller safe water access after sundown, on the final night of the holiday.

They'd gone to a party at one of his work friend's house. She'd noticed he was acting a little strange beforehand, but Greg was prone to moods, especially when it came to impressing his work buddies. It never occurred to her that he was planning to break up with her, let alone that he'd do it on the ride home.

Louisa sniffled as she took another sip of her expensive hot chocolate. It was way too sweet and piping hot, which was exactly what she needed. She'd thought to grab her purse when she demanded he pull over near the wharf, but she hadn't taken her coat. That left her in little more than a satin slip on the dark beach.

Even though San Francisco's winters were relatively mild, it wasn't exactly comfortable.

The hot chocolate burned as it slid down her throat, viciously sweet and thick as syrup. Not wanting to go back to her apartment to wallow just yet, she'd bought it from a cheerful vendor on the wharf who kindly ignored her smudged mascara and trembling chin. To the vendor, she was just one of many holiday tourists there to buy trinkets and ogle the twinkling lights strung up on moored boats. If anything, the lack of coat helped her. Only tourists walked around San Francisco unprepared for cool weather.

The atmosphere of the wharf was one of celebration — and absolutely intolerable to her.

Despite the fact that the Aquatic Park was only a few blocks away from the wharf, there was no else on the beach. She was entirely alone.

Staring at the yellow and orange light reflecting on the rippling surface of the water, she thought, *I can be fun.*

Maybe she didn't have the same interests as Greg's wealthy, globe-trotting friends, but that didn't mean she was *boring*. The people he aspired to be like used risk-taking and surface-level relationships with women who liked those things as status symbols. She didn't need to like rock climbing or motorcycles or skydiving to be interesting.

"I am interesting," she hissed, tears cooling on her cheeks. Swiping at her eyes, she shoved her paper cup into the sand. "I can be spontaneous. I can— I can do new things. Fuck Greg!"

Louisa stood up. Cool air slithered through the thin material of her green satin gown as she hurriedly slipped out of her stilettos. The sand was smooth and cool beneath her toes. It gave way as she hiked up her dress and began to march toward the waves.

She eyed the signs stuck into the sand that warned swimmers to stay within the borders of the park, helpfully illustrated with a picture of a merperson below waves. "Never done an ocean swim before," she muttered. "Never done a night swim either. I'm sure it'll be fine."

She knew it probably wasn't smart to get in the water when the temperature was so low, but she didn't intend to be in it for more than a moment. A few strokes and she'd wheel back around toward the shore, assured that she was brave and interesting and everything Greg said she wasn't.

Jaw firming, forced herself into the water.

"Oh, good *gods,*" she yelped, horrified by the sting of cold on her feet and ankles. San Francisco Bay wasn't exactly warm during the summer months, but during the winter it was downright frigid.

She danced back out reach of the waves almost as soon as she made contact. Hopping around in an attempt to bring some circulation back to her feet, she chanted, "No, no, no. Holy shit, no."

Louisa hugged her arms to her chest and turned back toward the shore. The sight of the lonely, steaming cup and abandoned stilettos in the sand stopped her in her tracks.

This wasn't about proving herself to Greg. He wasn't there, and she had no intention of speaking to him again.

This was about proving something to herself.

Louisa turned back around. Breathing fast, she grabbed two fistfuls of her dress and charged at the water with a fearless cry. That cry turned into something like a squeal when she crashed into the water. Millions of shards of ice penetrated her skin as she waded deeper and deeper into the sucking waves.

When it hit her chest, the cold squeezed the wind out of her lungs like a massive watery fist. She choked, gasping for air, but forced herself deeper. The soft sand slid between her toes as her dress dragged behind her, saturated with salty water.

Teeth chattering and nearly blinded by the pain of so much cold, Louisa slipped beneath a rolling wave.

It was absolutely the worst and stupidest thing she'd ever done. But she didn't turn back. She didn't want to.

When she came up for air the first time, pain gave way to numbness. Then numbness transmuted into a kind of bliss she'd never experienced before. A burst of euphoric laughter escaped her as she let the waves pull her closer to the blinking buoys that marked the border of the park.

The current was an invisible partner reeling her in for a dance. Louisa hadn't felt so alive in... maybe ever. The cold shocked her so much that she couldn't feel anything *except* alive.

She ducked under the waves again and again, splashing and kicking as her dress billowed around her in a dark green swirl. The closer she drew to the barrier, the more she could hear it under the water — the low hum of the underwater fence's defense system. There was another noise too, but she couldn't quite place it. A melody perhaps, but an alien one she'd never heard before.

She didn't dare touch the fence, and she knew that she ought to get back to the shore soon if she didn't want to end up with a nasty case of hypothermia, but since she was there, Louisa wanted to see what it looked like. That was what a daring, curious person would do.

Sucking in a deep breath, she ducked under a rolling wave and rolled her arms upward, pushing against the water to force herself down. Below the roar of the waves in her ears, the electrical hum grew louder and louder the closer she swam toward the fence.

And then there was that other sound — definitely a melody. A haunting one of many voices.

Many *close* voices.

Louisa's eyes sprang open under the water. Salt stung them, blurring her vision for a moment. But even through the haze, she could make out the bone-white faces staring back at her from beyond the shimmering barrier.

A gasp of horror forced her to suck in a lungful of briny water. Louisa choked and flailed as she blindly searched for the surface. It seemed like it took an eternity for her head to find it, but in reality it couldn't have been more than a few seconds.

Hacking up saltwater, she thrashed her arms against the current that no longer felt so gentle and inviting.

"It's a woman," she heard a peculiar voice note from the other side of the fence.

"Of course it's a woman," another one replied. "No man would be brave enough to swim here at night."

"Is she dying?" yet another asked with what appeared to be more mild interest than concern.

"I don't think so," the second voice replied. "Brave woman, are you dying?"

Brave woman? Louisa flinched as a wave bobbed her up and down aggressively. Wiping saltwater out of her stinging eyes, she squinted at the three pale faces staring back at her.

Merfolk. Her stomach dropped like a stone into the watery depths.

Wheeling backward like she had any hope of out-swimming three merfolk, Louisa babbled, "Um, I'm— I'm not— sorry, I'll just—"

"Not dying," the first voice announced. With a round face, big eyes, and dark hair braided back behind her ears, she appeared to be the oldest of the three.

They all seemed like adults, though Louisa couldn't say for

sure, seeing as she'd never met merfolk before. While they looked similar at first glance, they were actually very different. Their black and white facial markings were ever-so-slightly unique, and their features spanned the gamut of cherubic to aquiline.

"Oh good." The woman she recognized as the second voice gave Louisa a razor-sharp grin with a mouthful of deadly teeth. She had a variety of glass and shell beads woven into her hair, and while the other two hung back, she swam closer to the blinking buoy that marked the top of the fence.

"What are you doing out here, brave woman?" the beaded merwoman asked, not unkindly. "You don't seem dressed for the water."

Glancing down at the merwoman's bare breasts, she noted, "You don't seem dressed at all."

Louisa wasn't sure where the words came from, and she was humiliated the second they fell out of her chattering mouth.

There was a beat of silence before, as one, all three merwomen erupted into cackles. "This one has jokes," the third merwoman, who had shorn hair and wore a thick, corded necklace, exclaimed.

"You can take your dress off if you want to join us. I'm sure you have very nice breasts," the beaded merwoman offered. "And I would know. I *love* a good pair of breasts."

Louisa laughed and shook her head. "I'm— I think I'm good."

"Why are you out here? Hardly anyone swims in the park at night, and *no one* does it in the winter." The merwoman with the shorn hair pointed toward the glowing shape of the nearby wharf. Even from a few blocks away, the sounds of people and piped in music drifted across the water. "Were you watching the wharf? That's what we were doing."

Louisa couldn't say what compelled her to tell them the truth. Maybe it was the fact that she was in a vulnerable position, or perhaps it was the cold addling her brain. Either way, she found herself admitting, "I got broken up with tonight because I'm boring. Going for a swim felt like— it just felt like maybe it proved him wrong. I know it's stupid, but..."

All three merwomen's faces froze. Incredulous, the oldest one asked, "Your mate left you?"

"Well, we weren't officially..." Louisa shook her head. What did the details matter? "Yeah," she answered, voice raw from emotion and saltwater. "He left me."

Of all the things she could've expected from the three merwomen, it was *not* for them to explode into howls and begin thrashing the water with their arms and massive tails. Louisa recoiled, alarmed at the terrifying sight of three vicious predators' outrage.

Lunging for the fence, the beaded merwoman bellowed, "You should eat his liver!" Her black and white claws, thinly webbed between the fingers, curled around the buoy like it was Greg's thin neck. "You should eat his kidneys, too, so you get all the nutrients he doesn't use for his brain."

"You let him into your cove and he abandoned you? You should take your mating rope and string him up below the docks! Let the selkies have him," the older one called out, aghast.

The one with the shorn hair made a sucking sound behind her sharp teeth. Slapping the surface of the water with her palms, she growled, "Merfolk would never abandon a mate. This was your first mistake, brave woman. You should've chosen a strong mer."

The merwomen made a chorus of noises, some of which Louisa recognized as agreement. Shaking her head in astonishment, she kept her lips just above the water line as she mumbled, "I'm not a good fit for a merman, I think."

A series of scoffs made her cheeks heat despite the cold that was beginning to lose its euphoric effects.

"You're brave enough to swim in the ocean at night," the oldest one pointed out.

The beaded one gestured over her shoulder. "And my brother's mate is human. She's weak but he doesn't mind."

The one with the shorn hair gave her a look of deep concern. "You didn't give the weakling land-dweller pups, did you? A mer won't mind raising another's pups, but you should kill the father first before mating. It will save your new mate from having to do it to avenge his pup's honor."

"I don't think— Wait, merfolk kill people who leave their kids?"

The oldest merwoman flashed a terrifying snarl. "Abandoning pups means letting them die in the dark water or starve in a cove. It's a fitting punishment."

Louisa let another wave bob her like the buoy as she absorbed that troubling information. She'd known things were harsher under the water, but that was *harsh*-harsh.

Feeling a bit like she'd lost what little control she once had of the bizarre interaction, Louisa spat out a mouthful of salt-water before she answered, "Um, no. We talked about kids, but—"

If she wasn't so cold, she would've jumped at the second explosion of sound from the merwomen. At least this time it seemed to be one of approval rather than outrage.

"Then all is well," the beaded one exclaimed. "Once you eat his liver, you'll be full and ready to find a better mate to breed with when the season comes. We will help you."

Despite the growing stiffness in her limbs and the pain that was beginning to creep back into her skin, Louisa found herself laughing. "You're a lot nicer than I was led to believe. I thought you'd try to eat me, not find me a partner."

The one with the shorn hair flicked the water with a haughty sniff. "We only eat the weak and those who trespass. We *like* brave women who dare to swim at night. You'd do well in a pod. You're weak, but we would protect you."

The three merwomen nodded and made more of those strange melodic sounds.

Something warm bloomed in Louisa's chest despite the frigid water doing its best to send her into hypothermia. It felt a lot like acceptance — and there was nothing headier than the acceptance of women.

"Thank you," she rasped, arms swirling to keep herself afloat. "That... that really means a lot to me."

"Your lips are turning a strange color," the oldest one pointed out. "Is that supposed to happen?"

"N-no," Louisa chattered. "I probably need to get back to shore now."

"Come here for a moment, then you should go," the beaded one urged, waving her toward the buoy.

Feeling a bit like her limbs had increased in weight tenfold, Louisa forced herself to wade closer. The fence stood between them, barely visible beneath the dark water. She grasped the frigid metal of the buoy with numb fingers and waited for whatever it was the merwoman wanted to say.

All three drew closer. Placing their hands over hers on the buoy, they leaned as close to the fence they dared.

The strangest sense of togetherness made Louisa's chest go painfully tight when the beaded one whispered close to her ear, "We're friends now, brave woman. You can't be sad about your mate anymore. He's not worthy of you, and your pod would eat him if he were here."

The oldest one gave her wrist a gentle squeeze. "We will find you a better mate."

"And," the one with the shorn hair offered, "if you bring me his teeth, I will make them into a necklace for you."

"Wow," Louisa gasped, "I–I love th–that you do c–crafts. C–can you t–teach m–me?"

The one with the shorn hair puffed up with obvious pride. "I will teach you."

Overwhelmed by the camaraderie — a thing she'd never gotten before from her own people — Louisa fought back a wave of tears when she said, "I'm Louisa, by the way."

"Mary Celeste," the beaded one replied, gesturing to herself.

Pointing to the oldest one, then the one with the shorn hair, she introduced, "This is Lydia and Candace."

"I–it was r–really great to me–meet you tonight," Louisa said, with some difficulty. She offered the merwomen the strongest smile she could muster under the circumstances — mainly the brutal cold that was slowly stealing the life from her. "But I think I ha–have to go now or I–I'll die."

Like it was a funny joke rather than a very real thing that could happen, the merwomen released her hand with a laugh and shooed her back to shore.

"We'll see you soon, Louisa," they sing-songed in their strange, hypnotizing accent.

Forcing her limbs to work, Louisa began to doggy paddle back toward the sand. But not before she yelled over her shoulder, "M–may y–you find war–warmth on the da–darkest n–night!"

After all, it was a holiday, and as she stumbled blindly out of the water and into the sand, shaking uncontrollably and chilled to her very marrow, she knew for certain that they'd given her a gift better than any other.

Prairie Pack Party

He was a lucky bastard. There was no other way of putting it.

Viktor had no idea how he'd pulled it off, but he knew enough to be damn grateful for the gifts he'd been given.

It was the sound of pups playing in the snow that woke him from a perfect, dreamless sleep. White light filtered in through the backs of his eyelids as he rubbed his cheek against the smooth silk of the pillows Camille insisted were essential for her hair. Not that he put up a fight about anything she wanted, really. If he did, it was only because he wanted to see her get all riled up and triumphant when she "won" the argument later.

Truth was, he enjoyed her little decadences because they reminded him of her — his gorgeous, high maintenance alpha of an elf.

A smile curled his lips as he cracked his eyes open. The glare from the snow outside was intense, but he couldn't resist searching for the shape of his mate against the sea of white.

He knew the moment he woke that she wasn't cuddled into the sheets with him, but after the first instinctive flash of worry, there was only an aching sort of tenderness. His mate had abandoned their bed for a very good reason.

Prying himself out of bed, Viktor padded across the room to hook a finger around the edge of the gauzy curtain and pull it aside. Their yard sprawled before him, a landscape of snow and aspens. They'd gotten a fresh blanket of snow the night before, just after they put out the last Moonrise bonfire, but what he found wasn't the pristine white wonderland one might've expected.

Pawprints criss-crossed the mounds of snow and little hands had clearly been at work for some time trying to form a lopsided snowman. Tiny furry bodies wallowed in the powder, pink tongues lolling, while human-shaped children decked out in puffy snow suits attempted to make snow harpies.

Despite the adorable chaos, Viktor's gaze found Camille instantly.

Dressed in a stylish black coat and jaunty little beret, she was crouched in the snow near their fence helping some of the older children make snowballs. It took him a moment to understand why her coat fit her strangely: baby Bea, who wasn't *quite* so small as she'd been when they moved to Prairie, was strapped to her chest. Bea's little face stuck out from within the lapels like a little pink ball topped in a wool hat.

The tip of Camille's purple nose and cheeks had gone dark with the cold, which only highlighted the massive grin she sported. When Bea looked up at her with adoring eyes, they shared that smile like they were the best of friends.

Viktor let out a fond snort when he realized his mate had taken the time to put on *lipstick* before she intercepted the pups. Normally their den was overrun with the little ones first thing in the morning, but she'd obviously gone out of her way to keep them outside while he caught some extra sleep.

After the weeks of planning, construction, and meetings they'd had, he certainly couldn't complain about it. That didn't mean he'd miss another second of the fun, though.

And I need my good morning kiss, he thought, stepping back from the window with a growl.

After finding a long-sleeved shirt and a pair of jeans, he hunted down his boots. He didn't need all the protective snow gear that the little ones did, since adult shifters ran hot, but if he went outside without shoes on he was fairly certain his mate would flay him alive. Dressed just enough, he threw open the front door with a howl.

Immediately, every little coyote in his yard froze. Furry and hat-covered heads swivelled in his direction before, almost as one, they howled back with obvious delight.

"Good morning!" he cried, sinking into a crouch as a tide of little bodies descended on him. "You know, for the morning after Moonrise, you're all up *way* too early!"

Yips, barks, and the chatter of children all trying to talk at once made him grin. Someone attempted to drag him toward the lopsided snowman, a pup had somehow gotten their teeth into the heel of his boot, and another child wrapped their arms around his neck in a wordless request for a ride.

"All right, all right," he laughed, rising from his crouch. Someone dangled from his neck with a squeal of happiness, legs kicking, when he continued, "You know the rules! Cammie gets first kisses. I need to—"

He'd known Camille for a long time. He really should've expected the snowball to come flying at his face, and yet...

Viktor sputtered and wiped the slush from his eyes. Squinting, he found his beloved mate, the love of his life, the future mother of his children, the woman he'd die for without hesitation, standing across the yard with another snowball in hand and a mad smile on her lips.

"Oh, Alpha Hamilton wants a kiss, huh? You'll have to earn it!" Raising her right arm, she cried, "It's war!"

The children around him scattered with their own battle cries, and some of them dove for piles of snow to begin frantically making their own snowballs. Viktor ducked just in time to dodge Camille's projectile, which smacked their front door with a satisfying *splat!*

"No fair," he hollered, struggling to contain his laughter as he army-crawled for the cover of their shed. "You have a baby Bea shield!"

"A tactical advantage," she taunted, tossing another snowball with terrifying accuracy. He only just managed to dodge it by scrambling behind their shed's attached wood pile.

"Here I thought you just wanted to give me some extra sleep," he called out. "But this was your plan all along, wasn't it?"

"It's not my fault you're unprepared!"

Peeking out from behind the wood pile, he let out an amused puff of steam when he spied the battle that had broken out. Snowballs flew in every direction as children flung them with more enthusiasm than skill. The little ones in their coyote shapes sprinted back and forth, jumping high to nip at the balls as they flew above their heads. It was pure, blissful chaos.

Camille stood across the yard, a smug smile on her glossy lips and her gloved hands propped on her waist. Little Bea's content face peeked out from her lapels, a perfect defense.

Dodging wasn't an option. Neither was throwing a snowball. Even if she didn't have Bea, he wouldn't have done it.

There was only one choice.

Viktor charged into the fray with a howl. Snowballs pelted him from every angle as he became the main target of every child with a fistful of snow. He didn't stop. Viktor sprinted toward his mate, heedless of the frigid water seeping into his clothes, and snagged her around the waist with a satisfied growl.

Camille and Bea's laughter rang in his ears as he swept them both in a circle. "You're in trouble now, sweetheart," he warned, dropping his mate onto her fur-lined boots.

Cupping her flushed cheeks, he pressed a fierce kiss to her luscious mouth. Snowballs pelted his back, but he didn't care. Nothing could tear his focus from his mate when she gave him a sharp nip.

Whispering into his lips, she asked, "Good start to our first Burden's Moon?"

"The *best,*" he answered, stealing her beret and plopping it onto his own head. Pressing a kiss to the top of Bea's hat, he added, "But maybe warn a man next time, huh? It's just sporting."

Camille gave him one of those razor-sharp smiles he loved so much. "Don't count on it, alpha."

Shaking off the snow covering his back so it hit Camille, who shied away from the spray with a squawk, he thought again, *I'm one lucky bastard.*

Wolves in the Woods

Wolves got a bad rap. It was true, but it was also earned.

Juniper could admit that among shifters, they were usually the loudest, most boisterous, and leaned perhaps a little too close to arrogant. They also tended to run in large groups, which only made all those traits harder to ignore.

But for every less than stellar trait, she firmly believed that wolves embodied the very best of their kind.

Wolf packs rarely dissolved into bloodshed when alphas changed or circumstances necessitated that they split into new groups. They had some of the lowest rates of violence of any shifter type. They raised strong, honorable pups who knew how to laugh and how to protect.

And during the holidays, they knew how to throw a party.

Juniper tossed back her silver snout and let loose a jubilant howl as she raced her cousins through the trees of their territory. Sea cliffs lined one side of the forest and mountains the other. Beyond the cliffs lay the sparkly and deadly Bay, with its crown jewels of the Golden Gate Bridge and San Francisco beyond it.

Her pack owned most of Marin, which had been left wild and beautiful. Salt flats sprawled undisturbed, and the redwoods grew to enormous sizes from a lush carpet of ferns and native shrubbery. Only a small town and a scattering of cabins called the non-pack land home. The rest was theirs — and they loved every inch of it.

Juniper had grown up in the woods. She'd been a wild naked pup once, left to her own devices in the dense forest. She'd captured red salamanders in her tiny hands and sipped from free-flowing creeks before running home for dinner on four legs or two.

It was a perfect sort of life. Even as she grew and things became more complicated, as they tend to do with the onset of puberty, it'd never been a life she took for granted.

It was a special thing to be a wolf. And it was a perfect thing to be a wolf who was loved.

The soft fur of her cousins' pelts brushed up against her own as they dodged around tree trunks and nipped at each others' heels. They were a pack of several dozen now, four generations strong, and they danced together in the green undergrowth.

Patches of moonlight filtered in through the thick canopy, and every once in a while she'd break through near the edge of the cliffs to get a lungful of salty air. There was such wild joy in the annual run, in knowing nearly all her loved ones were experiencing the same moment with her.

Her parents were somewhere up ahead, no doubt nipping and yipping at one another flirtatiously like they were still caught in the mating fever, and even her grandparents joined in, though they stayed closer to the back. Nearly all her cousins had turned out, and only the youngest, sick, or otherwise unable to attend stayed back.

On the longest night of the year, they ran as one in the moonlight. Toward what, she couldn't say. The end wasn't the point.

It was the delight of togetherness on a night that otherwise might've been the loneliest. That was the destination, the goal, and the privilege.

Alashiya and Taevas Give Gifts

His queen had been in the kitchen all day, and that meant his Wing had been, too.

Taevas leaned against the door jamb to observe the scene. The kitchen in the guest accessible area of the roost was massive, as it was built to accommodate a fleet of cooks in the event of parties or other large gatherings. It still somehow managed to look crammed to the rafters with dragons hovering around his Chosen.

Alashiya, barefoot and dressed in a soft linen dress, moved between the cooker and the various stations set up around the marble countertops with the breathtaking grace that was so inherent to her. With her curls piled high on her head and secured with a silk scarf he'd given her just the night before — daily gifts had become something of a ritual for them, to make up for lost time — she looked beautifully at ease in a space that had once seemed so foreign to her.

And all around her were dragons.

"Don't over-mix that," she calmly instructed Pasha, who was absolutely over-mixing something in a large stainless steel bowl.

Pasha, with his broken horn and megawatt smile, gave Alashiya a bemused look. "How can you over-mix something, *kuninganna?* It's either mixed or it's not. And faster is always better, yes?"

"No," she answered serenely, with all the patience in the world for the dragon mixing so vigorously that the contents of the bowl had begun to splatter the counter. "When you mix flour, you develop gluten, which is what makes things bready. You don't always want that, right? We're making cookies, Pasha, not mini loaves."

Pasha's mixing slowed. Glancing at Alashiya with a hopeful expression, he waited for her to give him a thumbs up before he shot her his signature grin.

"Couldn't we use a mixer?" Aivar muttered. He was stationed by the stove, where he was meticulously leveling out scoops of powdered sugar before dumping them into a bowl.

"Doesn't taste the same," Alashiya and Radek answered simultaneously. The pair shared a knowing look as the rest of the dragons grumbled.

Radek, Alashiya's partner in crime, was armed with a knife, which he used to cut a massive bar of chocolate into thick shavings. His normally grim expression hadn't changed, but the line of his shoulders was always a little softer when he was with his Emand. The two were thick as thieves.

Taevas wasn't entirely certain Radek would hand over command of her security when the day finally came for Alashiya's own Wing to take up their post. They'd been vetting soldiers for months, trying to assemble the best of the best, but he had a feeling Radek would request that his position as Wing leader be made permanent.

He couldn't complain too much. If Radek wanted to make up for what he felt was a failure to protect his own mate by devoting his life to protecting Taevas's, then so be it.

In fact, he was pretty sure his *entire* Wing would've abandoned him for Alashiya if they could've. They did so whenever they got the opportunity, like today, when he'd been stuck in his office all day.

When they didn't have to worry about guarding him, they shot off like a pack of puppies looking for their mother. Even Roman, who was generally the least sociable of the group, was quietly moving cookies freshly out of the oven onto a cooling rack with his bare hands. Next to him, Vael and Hele had their heads bent together as they attempted to pipe what looked like white frosting onto crescent-shaped cookies, secret smiles on their faces.

And floating between them all was his Alashiya. The warmth of the busy kitchen made her cheeks a delightful dusky color, and the way her eyes lit up every time she gently corrected the technique or explained something to one of her workers made his chest tighten.

The smell of sugar and butter and his queen had lured Taevas from his office, but the sight of his closest friends gathered around his Chosen was better than any sweet.

Minu metsalill, you are a vision, he thought, wings twitching with the need to wrap her up tightly and whisk her away.

Alishya's head turned toward him as the hyphae channeled his affection and his need for her. A grin rounded her cheeks as she spied him by the door. "You're late," she scolded.

She padded across the kitchen on her bare feet, her dress fluttering in the sweet air, to greet him with a kiss that tasted like chocolate and cinnamon.

"My apologies," he replied, curling his tail possessively around her waist. "My meeting ran long."

"I'll forgive you this time. Did you bring the presents?"

Taevas held up the large bag she'd tasked him with fetching from her workshop. "Of course."

"Presents?" Pasha's voice carried across the room. "No one said anything about presents!"

"It's only a small thing," Alashiya demurred. Giving Taevas a nervous look, she reached for the bag. "Since I knew we'd all be baking today, I thought it might be nice if— Well, it's a little silly, but, um..."

He didn't like seeing her nervous, but no matter how many

times he'd assured her that her gifts would be a hit, she hadn't been able to shake the worry. In the end, he'd been forced to accept the fact that she wouldn't be reassured until she saw their reactions for herself.

So Taevas simply gave her a confident look and handed over the bag.

Alashiya kept her eyes down as she quickly flitted around the room, distributing small, cloth-wrapped packages to their intended recipients. "Taevas picked the colors," she babbled, practically shoving the last package into Radek's hands. "If you don't like them, I can make you another. It's really not a big deal. I just—"

Taevas crossed the kitchen to draw her into his side, interrupting her nervous rambling. "Open them," he ordered, giving the room a sweeping look. He didn't need to tell them to be nice, but it didn't hurt to give a little reminder.

The dragons didn't waste a moment. Carefully unwrapping their packages, they revealed what Alashiya had quietly been working on for the last several days: matching aprons she'd sewn for them and embroidered with silver moons and stars.

There was a moment of astonished quiet.

Alashiya paled, but just when her wide eyes swung toward Taevas with panic, a ripple of noise went around the room. Whoops of joy and whistles of appreciation filled the kitchen as everyone began showing off their gifts to each other, noting the colors and the fine craftsmanship of the embroidery.

No one appreciated textile work like dragons, and no one's skill was more appreciated than Alashiya's. It was legendary, after all.

Within moments, everyone had donned their aprons and crowded around her. The kitchen grew loud as everyone seemed to think it was necessary to talk at once, and in her excitement, Hele's sparks popped and sizzled in the air.

Alashiya self-consciously brushed a stray curl out of her eyes. "It's not a big—"

"You're very lucky to get a piece of my Chosen's work," Taevas interjected. Wrapping his tail around her wrist, he gave it a squeeze.

Hele slipped her green apron over her head. Vael circled behind her to tie it into a bow for her when she exclaimed, "I've never had an apron before! My Chosen, do you think I'm the first elemental to wear one?"

"Maybe," Vael answered, laughing. Taevas thought he looked half-decent in his own pale purple apron. "Elementals don't have much reason to wear them, I imagine."

"This one does," Hele chirped. "My cousin taught me how to bake!"

Alashiya wrapped her arm around Taevas's waist. He looked down to find her staring up at him, pleasure shining in her eyes. "Now I've just got to teach you," she teased. "Maybe you could start by helping Pasha with the cookie dough."

Pasha blew a raspberry and threw up his hands. Dressed up in his new pink apron, he hollered, "You can't over-mix cookie dough!"

A Very Fracture Holiday

Fracture didn't do holidays. For decades, any luxuries at all were entirely foreign to them, and there was nothing quite so luxurious as setting aside time to simply be... happy.

But times had changed. A tyrant was dead, they'd been given weekends off, and holidays could be enjoyed. Theoretically.

Of course, a gift was only as good as its usefulness, and unfortunately Fracture had no use for holidays.

That was exactly why Delilah thought it was time she took over. Her mother, Grim guide her soul, had once loved the solstices. Looking back, Delilah thought it might've been something of an escape for her to throw herself into the planning of elaborate events, the gifting of offerings to temples, and decorating what felt like the entire city.

Delilah left the religious and decorating parts of honoring her mother to Winnie. *Her* responsibility was making sure those who'd been forgotten for too long were brought into the light.

Or, more accurately, given an absolute banger of a Burden's Moon.

Her body practically vibrated with excitement as she sat in the passenger's seat of the blacked out military transportation vehicle.

Behind her, sitting with perfect stillness, were the helmeted members of Fracture — all of them.

She'd made sure to coordinate with Kaz and Valen to have all of them home for the start of the holiday. Like always, they thought she was nuts when she told them her plan, but they also agreed that if there was any way to give Fracture a holiday, this was probably it.

It wasn't a terribly long drive to their destination, but that was only the first half of their journey. No one asked any questions when she exited the vehicle at the dock in Marin and instructed them to do the same. The argument could be made that Fracture was too well trained to question orders, but Delilah knew that wasn't the case.

The truth was that Fracture did everything in their power to circumvent orders. It was a game to them, created out of the decades they'd been used and abused by her father as attack dogs. Every member constantly assessed a situation to find the cracks and loopholes that would give them a bit of power.

Once, that'd been necessary to save as many lives as they could. Now, it was mostly so they could get away with mischief.

So when she ordered them onto the small boat and no one said a word, Delilah knew it wasn't because they were blindly obedient. No doubt it had occurred to most of them that there was a possibility she was leading them to their execution and watery grave or something worse. They just knew that if murder at sea was on the docket, they'd get out of it.

One way or another, Fracture would survive.

Luckily for them and everyone she'd conscripted into helping her, she wasn't taking them out to sea for a tidy execution.

Delilah held onto the railing of the boat with her gloved hands, a wild grin on her face. The wet, salty air blew through her curly black hair and knocked the white fur-lined hood back onto her shoulders. The boat danced over choppy waves as they approached the tiny island.

They disembarked on what could only generously be called a

dock. Left to rot some fifty years ago alongside the rest of the buildings on the island, it was only barely capable of supporting their combined weight as they all jumped lithely over the ship's railing.

Turning to stand with the island behind her, Delilah tucked her hands behind her back and called out, "Attention!"

The black-clad members of Fracture snapped into formation instantly. Lining up shoulder to shoulder, they stood with their gloved hands pressed to their sides and their spines rigid, awaiting orders from their commander.

Looking over them all, Delilah felt something akin to pride. Not in their obvious fitness or that they were a powerful group of elves who'd do almost anything she told them to, but in their survival.

Against the odds, they'd all managed to outlive the bastard that'd made them.

"Fracture," she said, voice carrying over the crashing waves and the call of seabirds overhead, "you are being given an assignment."

Tilting her head toward the rundown buildings and island nearly overtaken by greenery, she continued, "In a moment I will board that boat. You will not. *You* will stay on this island for the next thirty days. The objective of your assignment is this."

Extracting a silver moon ornament from her pocket, she held it aloft. Winter sunlight glanced off its shiny surface, scattering light across Fracture's black visors and the creaky, swollen boards of the dock. The ornament dangled from a blue velvet string and swung gently from side to side like a hypnotist's watch.

"There are ten moons hidden on this island," she explained, watching the ever-so-slight tightening of shoulders and flexing of claws before her. "There are also supplies to last you the thirty days and caches of rewards, including but not limited to new weapons, video games, upgrades for vehicles, and more.

"However, alongside the supplies and gifts, there are also over one hundred traps designed by yours truly. I will return for you on day thirty. Whoever has the most moons on my arrival will be declared the winner of Burden's Moon and given a prize of their choosing — no limits."

There was very little that could excite Fracture into breaking formation but the promise of a game was high on the list.

The once perfectly straight columns of elves before her began to lose their shape as they shifted their weight. Their shoulders rounded and their heads lowered as they prepared for a hunt.

Instinct and excitement had begun to take over, as she knew it would.

Still holding the ornament in the air, she gave them a wild grin. "There are only three rules. First, no killing or maiming. Second, you may not leave the island. Third..." Delilah paused. Anticipation electrified the salty air as she looked at every visor-covered face in turn.

She didn't need to see them or even smell them to know exactly who was who. She'd grown up with these elves. She'd been trained by them and with them. They'd survived horrors beyond reckoning together, and she loved them with every fiber of her fucked up being.

Heart heavy with the weight of their bond, Delilah took a deep breath, turned on her heel, and chucked the moon ornament as hard and far as she could.

As it sailed through the air, she cried, *"Have fun!"*

Her hair and heavy violet cape flapped as the elves bolted by her, nearly too fast for the naked eye to see. A gleeful burst of laughter exploded from her lips as she watched her friends race down the abandoned dock. Some went after the ornament she'd thrown, but others immediately split off, headed for the old shipping warehouse she'd filled with traps or the crumbling lighthouse she'd *also* filled with traps.

Confident she'd finally found a way for them to enjoy the holiday, she briskly rubbed her gloved hands together and strode back toward the boat. As much as a part of her wished to join them in the madness that was to come, Winnie was waiting for her.

Someday they'd all understand what a gift it was to be loved, but for now, this would just have to do.

A Snowy Goodeland

The dock was far away from the revelry of the Moonset celebrations, and that was exactly what Margot needed.

It wasn't that she didn't want to spend time with her family, but sometimes it got to be just... too much. There were too many people. There was too much noise. There was too much otherness.

That last one was the worst.

Margot wrapped the blanket she'd pilfered from the house around her shoulders and exhaled a slow breath. It clouded in front of her, a little puff of fog that briefly obscured her view of the ice-crusted lake. The sound of instruments and squealing children's laughter were a faint song in the frozen night, and the scent of bonfire smoke clung to every breath she took.

It'd been nice to be a part of the celebration for a while. She'd played with her cousins, ate her fill, and made her offering to the fire when her turn came. But she never lasted longer than a couple hours at events like Moonset. Lately it felt like that timeline had shrunk.

Noni Tula said it was a normal part of becoming a teenager, that sense that she just didn't belong, but Margot wasn't so sure. It wasn't just otherness.

It was a slow strangulation.

She sniffed, eyes stinging, and drew a corner of the blanket up to her lips. Snow had begun to fall from the dense clouds overhead. She watched as the flakes spiralled in the air before they landed on the frozen water. They fell on her, too, until the top of her head and blanket-covered shoulders were dusted white.

It didn't surprise her when soft footsteps crunched the snow behind her. Alric was good about giving her space, but he never let her stew for long. It was like he had a sixth sense for when she needed company.

The lanky teen quietly dusted off the other folding chair that sat at the end of the dock. Dressed in a smart black coat with green gloves and a matching scarf, he would've blended in with the adults if not for the softness of his cheeks. Even that was changing every day, though. Sometimes she imagined that he grew an inch every night, trading his baby fat for height.

She hated him for it. Just a little.

Growing up seemed so effortless for him and all the others, while for her it was a constant battle. The healers said she probably wouldn't get any taller than she was, and putting on weight was almost impossible, which meant she wasn't developing like her cousins. While her cousin Ruby had blossomed into a curvy, vivacious young woman practically overnight, Margot was stuck with knobby knees, no breasts, and being asked for parental permission to get into PG-13 movies rather than out on dates.

Everyone around her was changing while she remained as she'd always been: stuck.

"Here," he said, holding out a steaming paper cup.

Margot exposed as little of her hand as possible to accept it. Unlike her cousin, she hadn't thought to bring her gloves or hat out with her.

"Thanks," she whispered. Her fingers burned a little when she wrapped them around the cup, but it was a good kind of burn. Bringing it up to her lips, she took a small sip of the spiced cider.

Sweetness washed over her tongue, shortly followed by the spice of the cinnamon stick he'd thoughtfully included.

Alric made himself comfortable in his chair. One thing she liked about him was that he never rushed into speaking. Her cousin was perfectly at ease with silence, just as she was.

Even though they'd only lived together for a short time, she'd come to think of him as something like a brother. It was rare that they didn't share the same opinion, and their habits were strikingly similar. But Alric had a quiet confidence that she lacked.

More importantly, perhaps, he had the freedom to act on it.

Margot took another sip of her cider, trying to wash the thought down. Glancing at her cousin out of the corner of her eye, she noted his faraway expression as he gazed out at the still lake.

"Nice night," she noted, turning her own eyes back to the snow.

Alric hummed. "Storm's coming in."

"How'd you know that?"

"I can taste it," he answered, sounding very sure of himself. "Also, Sophie mentioned it earlier."

Margot snorted into her cider. "Some nose you've got there."

"Don't be rude. I brought you cider."

"I already said thank you, didn't I? What more do you want?"

Alric crossed his arms over his chest and leaned back in his chair. It creaked a little under his weight. "You coming back to the party?"

"Probably not," she admitted.

She braced herself for questions, but he didn't ask why. Maybe he didn't need to.

"I don't want to go back either," he sighed.

It was perhaps a little hypocritical of her, but Margot replied, "You should. Grandma wants to introduce you to everyone, remember? It's important that you start—"

"Developing relationships," he finished with her. "I know.

But I've been doing nothing but talk to old people for hours. I need a break."

She could hardly blame him for that. Margot wasn't particularly envious of Alric usurping her place as Sophie's heir on a good day, but she was especially glad about it when she saw just how much handshaking and polite nodding it required.

"You can stay out here with me," she generously offered.

She caught Alric's smile out of the corner of her eye. "I appreciate it. I know how much you like your alone time."

Margot wasn't sure if she *liked* it so much as she *needed* it. With a family as big and tangled as theirs, and with her problems as... unique as they were, sometimes the only way to tolerate it all was to run away.

She took another long sip of her cooling cider as she waffled over whether she ought to say something to him or not. In the end, it was the cider itself that prompted her to climb the barrier of her self-consciousness.

Taking a deep breath, she haltingly admitted, "Yeah, well... Having you around is pretty much the same as when I'm alone, so I don't mind too much."

Alric's head turned to look at her. For such a young man, he had very a serious face. It was another thing they shared — that thing in them that people seemed to recognize as being too old, too knowledgeable, and too sad for their age.

Margot silently held out the cup.

Her cousin accepted it slowly and brought it to his mouth for a sip. Breath puffing from his lips, he said, "You aren't too bad to have around either, you know."

Figuring now was as good a time as any to ask him for the thing she'd been agonizing over, she muttered, "Can you do me a favor?"

She could almost feel Alric's focus honing in on her like the beam of a spotlight. He was always so calm that his bursts of intensity sometimes took her by surprise. "What do you need?"

"It's nothing important," she quickly assured him. Her voice was slightly muffled as she pulled the blanket back up to her lips.

"Tell me."

Fighting the urge to take it all back and tell him to forget about it, she forced herself to explain, "So, the first day of my apprenticeship is Monday and… I was wondering if you could drive me there. And— and there's a welcome breakfast for family if you wanted to maybe stay for a bit."

Alric's dark brows furrowed as he digested her request. "Isn't Sophie going to drive you? Or Tula?"

"Noni's flying out to visit her family that day, and Grandma…" Margot trailed off, something in her seizing. When she continued, her voice was soft and small. "I don't want her to see how nervous I am."

"Oh." He was quiet for a long moment, his expression contemplative. "And you want *me* at this breakfast thing?"

"You don't have to go if you don't want to," she rushed to assure him. "It's just a stupid welcome party. There'll be some speeches and all the other apprentices there with their families and—"

And they'll all be ten years older than me at a minimum. And they'll have their loved ones there to really celebrate them rather than worry about them. And I really, really don't want to sit through it all alone.

"—it's really not important," she finished, looking anywhere but at him.

Alric crossed his ankles in front of him. Offering her the cider once again, he quietly replied, "Well, if it's not important then I should *definitely* go. If we don't show up for the stupid shit, then what's the point of family?"

Margot swallowed hard. She wasn't sure when her throat started hurting, but it smarted something terrible just then.

Delicately extracting the cup from his fingers, she used the need for another drink as an excuse to hide just how much his casual acceptance meant to her. Looking down at the snow whispering across the frozen water in little white swirls, she mumbled into the paper lip, "Cool. Right. Yeah."

Beside her, Alric tilted his head back onto the folding chair. They were quiet for a while as they listened to the creak and pop of the ice below the jubilant party sounds.

In a quiet, content voice, her cousin noted, "Really is a nice night, huh?"

"Yeah," she answered, hugging the cup close. "It really is."

Back home in the Holler

The rumor in town was that cousin Silas was crazy, but Annie Dupont knew better. He was crazy *and* he was right.

Technically speaking, they weren't really cousins. Her parents weren't officially Cuttcombes, but they'd been neighbors with the rowdy clan for so long that no one paid much mind to things like that. She'd grown up as a member of the clan, and that meant she knew a thing or two about Silas. She also knew what people whispered at school.

He talked to imaginary friends.

He liked to set things on fire.

He shouldn't be left alone with anyone, even the older boys, because you never knew what he'd do.

All of these things were, in fact, true. But they didn't mean what folks thought they did.

"Why are you crying?" Amber on black eyes stared down at her with the same curiosity she imagined scientists showed when they picked apart a bug to see how its insides worked.

Silas, dressed in overalls and leather boots with his book bag slung over his shoulder, stood over her as she frantically attempted to stuff wrapped parcels back into the brown paper bags her mother had given her to deliver.

While she was bundled up all the way to her horn nubs, he dressed much the same as he did all year. The only difference was that he wore a light sweater beneath his patched overalls rather than the starched linen his mama made him wear in the summer.

Annie swiped her running nose over her wool sleeve. Her knees were getting cold. They hadn't gotten much more than a dusting of snow yet, but that was enough to soak through her stockings as she scrambled to save her mother's hard work.

"Ed tripped me," she muttered. "He saw me walking with my arms full of orders and..."

Her chin wobbled. Embarrassed by her tears, she looked away. Ten was far too old to be a baby, especially in front of cousin Silas.

Her cousin didn't stoop to help her, but he didn't grunt and walk away like most boys would've, either. Instead, he asked, "Does he do that a lot?"

Annie shrugged. Truth be told, Ed *did* do that a lot. She was normally better about not letting the teasing or poking or hair-pulling get to her, but today was different. The holiday was only a few days away, and her mother worked herself to the bone in the bakery every year to fulfill all the orders for Moonrise treats.

All Annie wanted to do was help where she could. This year, that meant finally being trusted with helping deliver orders. To have Ed come along and laugh as he tripped her, making her scatter all that hard work into the dirt, was more than she could stomach.

Carefully dusting off the last paper-wrapped loaf of bread with her gloved fingers, she straightened up. Her mama charged her with a job, and by Blight, she'd do it.

"Why do you let him do that to you?"

"What do you mean?" The bag crinkled as she placed the loaf inside and rolled the top back up, keeping the baked goods from the snow drifting lazily down on their heads.

"Why don't you make him stop bothering you? I see him doing it at school. He's very annoying."

Annie snorted. Climbing to her feet, she replied, "He's twice my size. If I fought back, he'd beat me to a pulp."

"He's beat you?"

Something in Silas's voice made her look up sharply. The hair rose on her arms and the back of her neck when she looked into his familiar face.

Folks said he was a pretty boy. He took after his healer daddy, with his freckles and his nice smile, but he had his mama's dark horns and eyes. His chocolate curls fell across his forehead in a way that she envied, since her hair was the same color and about as interesting as under-baked bread. But his good looks didn't hide the thing that made all those rumors swirl.

Silas was scary.

Shadows crept along his body at all times, more alive than any she'd seen, there was a light in those amber eyes that often seemed unnatural, and, of course, he spoke to ghosts.

The dead sought him out, she heard old folks say, usually followed by a quick prayer to the Merciful One. They lingered around him, attracted to something strange and uncanny in his soul, and that was why his shadows were so different from everyone else's.

Outside of the clan and in the schoolyard, people said that he was crazy. She didn't respect it. If they felt a certain way about his *imaginary friends*, they ought to say it loud. But they were scared of Silas, so when they smeared Grim's mud across his name, they *whispered,* too afraid to tease him in a louder voice.

And they were wrong about his friends being imaginary. She knew that because she'd seen them. She was one of the very few cousins who dared spend any time with him after dark, when the wraiths came alive.

So when Silas looked at her like that, with that flat, predatory stare as his shadows licked across his face like a hungry snake, she knew enough to be truly afraid.

It was a confusing thing, feeling a deep and instinctive fear of someone she'd shared baths with.

Annie loved her cousin to the bone. They were a loyal sort, demons. Once you got in their hearts, there wasn't much to be done about it save surrender to it.

But she was afraid all the same.

"Yes," she whispered, hugging the bag close to her chest. Her own shadows were a nervous flutter beneath her skin, like a second heartbeat. "He corners me on my walk home. Usually he just throws rocks and things, but sometimes he pulls my hair or hits me."

Silas blinked slowly. "Are you headed back home?"

Brows furrowing, she replied, "Um, after I drop off these orders. Why?"

"Can you take my book bag with you?"

"...Sure, I s'pose," she agreed. "Why? You stopping somewhere? If you wanna get your parents a Moon Gift, you ought've done that already. The corner store's nearly out of everything good."

Slipping the strap of his leather bag over her shoulder and carefully adjusting the weight to account for her full arms, he said, "I already got my mama earrings and I made my daddy a pair of bookends."

When his bag was all settled and she adjusted her grip on the baked goods, she gave him a curious look. "So what are you doing, then?"

Silas gave her one of those smiles that made folks talk about how he wasn't quite right. "Get on home now, Annie. Tell your folks I said hi, all right?"

Giving a jaunty salute, he turned on his heel and began trotting in the opposite direction of home. Snow caught in his curls and the top curves of his horns as he stuffed his claws in the pockets of his overalls.

Stomach sinking, she called out, "Si, don't do anything too bad, would you?"

"I never do bad," he replied, as calm as anything. "I only do just right."

Annie wasn't so sure about that, but she didn't have time to be worrying about what Silas might or might not do. Even if she could've stopped him from doing whatever it was he got into the space between his horns, she had deliveries to make.

So she trudged along, her knees cold and wet but her spirit a little less bruised than before. When the last of the bread, buns, and sweet little cakes had been delivered, she did as she'd been asked and dropped his book bag off with his daddy, who offered her a cup of cocoa to go — after he healed a scrape on her elbow, of course.

And if she heard a familiar-sounding voice let loose a scream while she sipped it on her way home... well, that was none of her business. Her job was done.

Man on the Mountain

Soren liked a lot of things about living alone on a mountain. The views were good, the air was clear, and there was no one around to bother him — including his pushy sister.

"You're seriously not coming?" Vanessa complained.

"I'm seriously not coming," he grunted, propping his feet on the polished log he used as a stool. Fire crackled in the hearth he'd built with local stones, and stew bubbled away on the stove behind him, steaming the air with the scents of sage and venison.

"You know, it wouldn't kill you to come to the city for five minutes."

Adjusting his grip on his phone, he used his other hand to pick up his beer and bring it to his lips. "Mm," he muttered into the bottle, "might."

"It *wouldn't,*" she insisted. "You would stay at my *luxurious penthouse.* Be *wined* and *dined* by the finest San Francisco society has to offer. All for the low, low price of coming to my Moonrise party."

Soren lifted his brows and peered at the knitted toes of his socks. The bottom of his feet tingled with the warmth of the fire. "I happen to think my accommodations are plenty luxurious."

His sister's sigh came through loud and clear through the

phone. "Soren, people think I've made you up. I already told my friends you're coming. Please just come to my damn party."

Wiggling his warmed toes, he offered, "What if I send you a card?"

"A card? Seriously?"

He hummed. "I could send some jerky for the party."

"The party's going to be catered by one of the best chefs in the city." Vanessa paused, let out a sigh, and added, "But I would like some of your jerky. For me."

Smiling into the rim of his beer, he assured her, "I already put some in the mail for you. And some huckleberry jam."

Slightly mollified by this news, his sister turned down the urgency somewhat when she said, "That's not much of a replacement for your company, you know. Has it occurred to you that maybe I just miss seeing your stupid face? We haven't seen each other since Mom's exhibit."

And that was more than enough.

Soren set his beer down with a soft sigh. Guilt tightened his gut, but it wasn't enough to make him lose his mind and actually agree to spending a week in San Francisco.

He loved his sister. He really, really did. No one in the world understood him better than Vanessa.

But in many ways they were very, very different.

There were no rules to being a were — especially not for them, the first generation born into it.

While Vanessa had inherited plenty of shifter traits from their father, socially she took a lot more from their mother's side. She thrived amongst throngs of people and in the cut-throat art world. When she encountered obstacles, she took great pleasure in ripping them to pieces with ruthless cunning and strategy. Being an alpha meant something very different to her than it did to him.

Soren was... more bear than anything else.

Despite the colors of his eyes and the gland in the roof of his mouth, he was his father's son: a solitary polar bear.

He couldn't shift, but he could feel the bear in ways his sister couldn't, and that meant their tolerances for things were very different. He couldn't handle the noise and the smells and the crowds of the city. He wanted to roam his mountain and hunker down in his cozy den, not let his sister squeeze him into a suit so she could introduce him to her rich friends.

But that wasn't a kind thought.

Vanessa wasn't shallow. She was an intelligent, driven, powerful woman making changes in the world he didn't have the stomach to fight for. Soren was fucking *proud* of his sister.

And he did miss her. Even when she was pushy.

"Has it occurred to you that I have a guest room?" he shot back. His eyes, one a dark blue and the other a pale green, rested on the empty armchair beside his. "Get away from the city for a while. We can roam and cook and maybe you can actually get some sleep for once."

Vanessa let out a long sigh. "I've got too much work to disappear in the mountains for a week."

"Then it appears we're at an impasse," he replied, flicking a lock of long blond hair out of his eyes.

"There's really nothing I can say to get you to come?"

"Nope."

His sister blew a raspberry into the phone. "Fine! Disappoint your sister. *Again.*"

"Keep an eye on your mail," he reminded her.

"Yeah, yeah." After a brief pause to really make sure he felt her disappointment in him, she added, "I'll plan to visit you next month, okay?"

Soren's fanged smile widened. "Looking forward to it, cub."

"Love you, you big dumb bear."

Snagging his beer again, he brought it up to his lips. "Love you. Don't forget to call Mom."

"She'd come to my party," Vanessa grumbled.

Pulling the phone away from his ear, he called out, "No, she wouldn't," before he ended the call. Brotherly duties accomplished, he tossed his phone onto the side table, took a large swig of his beer, and closed his eyes — a bear content in his den, ready to take on whatever winter threw at him.

Sisters Celebrate

"I'm jus—just *saying,*" Atria slurred, "I don't think it would be *hard.*"

Ruby blinked owlishly up at the cascade of bubbles that made up her chandelier. Every time her eyes opened, the lights changed color. That was what she wanted to happen. What she *didn't* understand was why the lights appeared to move on their own.

"I didn't put my lights on servos, did I?" she muttered, squinting.

"Servos?" Atria's head lifted from the satin pillow she'd commandeered from the couch. Snickering, she gave her butt a wiggle. "Servos this *ass.*"

Ruby blinked again, changing the lights from green to pink. The ever-present hum of electricity was comforting to her even in her horrifically inebriated state, but the pathways she normally so easily accessed to control the technology around her were a little harder to figure out. "I'm serious. Are the lights moving or is that the vodka?"

"S'definitely the vodka," Atria answered.

Relieved that her lights weren't actually spinning, Ruby turned on her side to hunt for the bag of cookies they'd pilfered from the department Moonset party. Broke college students couldn't be expected to *not* steal from the buffet table, so she didn't feel too bad about the theft.

"Maybe whatever was in the cider," she muttered, fingers crawling across the carpet like a ring-clad spider. "Or the jello shots."

"Think that's also vodka," her friend pointed out. Smacking her palm on the floor, she exclaimed, "But that's not important!"

Atria's long hair proved to be an obstacle to Ruby finding the bag of treats they'd stolen. Swiping the dark strands out her way, she spied the bag mostly crushed beneath the satin pillow. "Wus important?" she mumbled, intent on extracting the crinkly iridescent plastic bag without moving more than two fingers.

Atria flopped her arms and legs out across the living room floor. The hundreds of tiny silver moon sequins covering her short dress scattered the pink light across the room. Her slurred voice was made even less understandable by the fact that she had most of her face smushed into the pillow when she explained, "Adoption! I don't think it's *hard.*"

Letting out a whoop of triumph when her fingers hooked on the shiny edge of the bag, it took Ruby's alcohol-soaked brain a second to catch up to what she'd said.

Making a face, she replied, "Adoption? You wanna have a kid? Dude, you've never even had a *pet.* Try a cat first or something."

While Ruby dragged the bag across the carpet toward her greedy mouth, Atria moaned, "Nooo. I'm talking 'bout a *sister* adoption."

"Sis'er 'doption?" The words didn't come out quite right mostly because she'd finally succeeded in shoving a silver sprinkled, crescent moon-shaped cookie into her gob. Crumbs spraying, she mumbled, "Don' thin' thassa thing, 'Tria."

"It so is," her friend argued, tattooed arms flailing.

"So isn't." Deciding she was tired of the pink light, Ruby glanced up at the slowly moving chandelier and blinked twice, changing its color to violet then teal.

Atria sat up on her elbows to give her a wounded look. The

effect of it was somewhat hampered by the veil of dark hair that'd fallen across her face, not to mention the smeared eyeliner and body glitter. "You don't wanna be my sister?"

Digging around the bag for another cookie, Ruby replied, "I wanna, but I just don't think it's *legal* is all."

"Oh." Atria looked truly crestfallen, which wouldn't do.

Pushing her bare feet into the carpet, Ruby scooted herself toward her friend on her back. "Doesn't mean we can't be sisters," she offered, holding out the bag full of crushed holiday cookies. "We just gotta do it criminal style."

Ruby shook the bag. "We'll be cookie sisters. Cookies exist beyond the bounds of the *law.* Those are for measly men and cookie-haters."

"Oh," Atria breathed, nodding. It took her two tries to get her aim right, but eventually she managed to get her fingers in the bag. Breaking off a piece of already shattered cookie, she offered it to Ruby with all the solemnity of the temple priestess she'd been raised to be.

"Cookie sisters," she intoned, "from now until death!"

Ruby took the piece and brought it to her lips. "From now until death!" After some thoughtful crunching, she added, "Or until I throw these up later."

Atria flopped back down onto her pillow. *"Puh-lease* don't talk about throw-up."

Fairylight 24hr Books

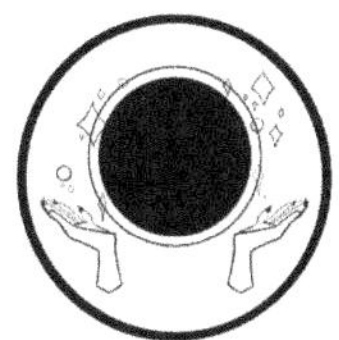

Margot didn't feel at home at very many places in San Francisco. Even after two months in the city, she struggled to get used to being so alone and yet constantly surrounded by strangers. With the looming holiday, she felt that isolation much more keenly. And that was saying something, because she *always* struggled during Burden's Moon.

There were only two places she felt at ease. The first, of course, was her clinic. The second was the bookstore.

Fairylight 24hr Books was empty when she stepped through the old doors, the bell over her head chiming. The bookshop was almost oppressively warm, as if all the books crammed so tightly together on the shelves that spiderwebbed out from the entrance were somehow creating their own heat. Upbeat jazz whined from the tinny speakers mounted in the corners of the store. Claudette, the giantess who owned The Fairylight, refused to play anything else.

The Fairylight was willfully against city coding, organization, and common sense. The store was a maze of towering bookshelves and uneven floorboards covered in old, mismatched area rugs. The electricity hadn't been updated since the thirties, so exposed wiring snaked along shelves and what little could be seen of the walls, trailing up into light fixtures that glowed orange.

Margot, who'd spent most of her spare time in the shop since she discovered it, still couldn't make heads or tails of the place.

"Bardil?" she called, adjusting her hold on the paper coffee cups in her hands, "Claudette?"

"In history, healer."

Margot ran a hand through her windswept hair, her fingers caught in the tangles as she wound her way through the stacks. The Fairylight was probably the only place in San Francisco one could walk right by a giant and not see them.

Claudette was hunched over a rusty cart, her huge, arthritic fingers plucking up books by the tens. Margot nearly passed right by her, tucked away as she was in the moving shadows cast by the buzzing lights. Seeing the giant was always a pleasure, but it was particularly nice on that rainy Sunday.

Turning her great head to look at Margot through coke-bottle glasses, her cloud of white hair swaying, Claudette asked, "Everything all right there, healer?"

Margot offered her friend the coffee she'd picked up from Ruffled Feathers. When Claudette took it between two fingers, Margot unzipped her jacket with her free hand, letting in the musty warmth. Looking up at her elderly friend, the words came out in one gust. "I didn't get much sleep last night."

"You look it. Did the clinic get busy?"

Margot shook her head. "No, I just had a less than sane idea last night."

The giantess' fingers stilled on the shelf. Her eyebrows, white bushy things that stuck out above her lenses, pinched on her wrinkled forehead. "What? You planning a coup or something? The elves won't take kindly to that, I tell you what."

"What? No." She shuddered. "I could never run this territory."

"Then what? Are you planning a murder?"

Margot watched Claudette turn her attention back to the

shelf. "No," she answered, already flustered. "I just— I went to the market off of Carolina Street the other day, and I noticed... Well, you remember when we were talking about how there used to be a clinic in there when I came by last week?"

"Ah." Claudette's old bones creaked as she roughly scooted books to one side, making room for newcomers. Margot never once caught her actually organizing a pile of books, but somehow they were always in order by the time they made it to the shelf. "So you bought contraband."

"Huh? No! What would I even do with— I *want* to reopen a clinic there. You know, for all the people who can't or won't go somewhere—"

"Ah, ah! This sounds like it'll take a while. If you're going to chat, you're going to work." Claudette jabbed a meaty finger at a stack of paperbacks on the cart, saying, "You know the drill, healer. No free rides in this bookshop. You buy or you work."

Taking a long draw from her coffee, Margot nodded. She didn't mind being put to work, just as Claudette had never minded telling her what to do. She'd had Margot shelving books halfway through their first conversation, when she wandered in looking for more vintage sci-fi paperbacks.

Real paper books weren't terribly common, so when she found a shop that sold them in abundance, she never passed up the chance to find treasures. It was a lucky thing that she found a friend inside, too.

Hefting the stack into the crook of her elbow, Margot prowled the section to find the proper places. She could alphabetize. She could artfully arrange. She could get her over-excited thoughts in order.

Words tumbled out of her as she worked, painting a rough picture of what she's spent the entire night planning. It'd been a welcome break from the panic and fear that clawed at her in the dark, made all the worse by the looming holiday — which might very well be her last.

Claudette listened dutifully to her rambling, interrupting her only once to offer help with a tall shelf.

When she'd finished, the giantess made a thoughtful sound and summarized, "You want to open a secret clinic. That doesn't seem so bad. The city might have a problem with it, mind, if they discover you're pilfering supplies, but who cares what they think? They've been trying to shut me down for code violations for nearly a hundred years."

Margot stared at the nearly empty cart, her filed nails worrying the peeling black paint on the handle. She shook her head. "I know it's not that daring. I just... I've never done anything rebellious in my life. I don't think I've ever even broken a rule."

"You came here all on your own," Claudette pointed out.

Because I'm running out of time, she silently replied. The clock was ticking not just for her to find her bondmate, that faceless person who'd save her life, but to be *useful.* To be anything of worth at all.

"I want to help people," she sighed. "And I just don't feel like I'm doing that in the St. Francis Woods healing house. Not enough."

Claudette snorted. "Then do it." Her glasses slid down the length of her nose, but were saved from an untimely descent by the bulbous, rosy tip. Claudette reached out to tweak the round ear that peeked out from behind Margot's red hair, a toothy smile crinkling the skin around her eyes. "You've got good instincts. Use them, huh?"

"It does *feel* right," she admitted, a familiar certainty settling in her gut. It was the same feeling that had drawn her relentlessly toward San Francisco. That had to mean something.

Right?

A hot puff of air stirred her hair. Margot looked up, startled to find Claudette was rolling her eyes at her. "What?" she asked, baffled.

The giantess waved a huge hand dismissively. "You're a *witch,*

Margot. And you're a young, beautiful, single one at that. It's unnatural to be so unsure of yourself. Straighten your shoulders and get out in the world already. It's waiting for you."

Slinging a heavy arm over her shoulders, Claudette gave her a reassuring, bone-crushing squeeze. "Drink your coffee," she sternly ordered. "Then grab another stack of books. Burden's Moon is coming. Do you have any idea how much stocking I have to do to get ready for all the gift-giving?"

Pixie Feeding Fortunes

"Pixies: Pests, Predictions, and Perseverance" by Elise Sasini for *The San Francisco Light*, published 21 December 2048

Where there are people, there are pixies. And where there are pixies, there are traditions as old as the creatures themselves.

Caeruleosalatus brevimanus, more commonly known as the domesticated pixie, originated from a now extinct wild species native to Europe, Asia, and North Africa. Bred some 10,000 years ago to select for friendliness and navigation, pixies are the small, blue, winged companions to the rise of civilization. If you've ever visited a city or hung out beneath an overpass as a wayward teen, then you've certainly seen your fair share of pixies.

In case you didn't spend your adolescent years ditching class to hang out beneath bridges like I did, then you might not have gotten up close and personal with the blue creatures who hide in the cracks and crevices of the modern world. Even so, you've heard of them.

Pixies don't just populate attics or make nests out of stolen socks. For generations, they were the sole means of communication between far-flung communities, with messages of love and loss and warning carried in their little blue hands. It was a mighty responsibility for creatures so small, and perhaps that's why so many superstitions sprang up around them.

When the days are dark and food runs scarce, a lowly pixie carrying a message might be the only creature standing between your community and death. Today, many of us have forgotten days of famine and fear, but cultural memory runs deeper than any one person. Stories linger. Traditions, particularly those tied to the survival of winter, are ingrained in our collective DNA.

Pixies star in many Burden's Moon stories. Their images decorate children's books explaining the importance of hearth and home. Songs about mischievous pixies stealing gifts only to leave better ones in their place dominate the airwaves.

Our forgotten lifelines are everywhere during the thirty days of Burden's Moon. To pixie enthusiasts like Dr. Moira Luten, a biologist and pixie expert from San Francisco Protectorate University, they're important year-round. I sat down with her for a coffee to discuss her favorite subject and watch the frenzy of activity that is Union Square being decorated for the holiday.

Dr. Luten doesn't look like what you might imagine a typical biologist would. Short, curvy, and dressed to the nines, she has a dreamy smile and a calm demeanor that's a breath of fresh air to your reporter, who's been stuck in the bullpen for a little too long.

While we make ourselves comfortable on the bench, she asks, "So, what do you think of pixies?"

Normally in an interview, I'm the one asking the questions, so it takes me a moment — and a too-hot sip of my latte — to summon an answer.

"To be honest, I don't have much of an opinion. I like them well enough, I guess, as long as they aren't chewing holes in my walls," I answer.

"Pixies don't chew holes," she corrects me. Lifting one hand, she makes a scratching motion in the air. "They dig them. Their claws are made of a similar material as elvish claws, which makes them incredibly efficient little homemakers."

"I just wish they wouldn't make so many homes in my drywall," I reply, half-joking.

Dr. Luten gives me a long look as she sips her drink — a coma-inducing mixture of syrups, foams, and non-dairy milks I can barely comprehend. Sensing judgement, I rush to add, "I mean, I think they're cute, but they're also pretty loud."

"That's because they communicate through song," she explains. "They have an incredibly advanced language, actually. Studies have shown that they create new 'words' for unknown things, and that they pass them on to their flights."

A *flight* is a group of pixies, and the study she's referencing is actually one she co-authored five years ago. It showed that pixies have a vocabulary, and that while different flights have unique songs, they also share enough common language that when two pixies from completely different groups meet, they can effectively communicate.

The reminder that they're intelligent, if loud, little creatures makes me a little abashed. I rub my neck as I try to find a way to redeem myself. It's too early in an interview to be so wrong-footed.

"I don't love loud neighbors, but I've been a fan of pixies since I was a kid," I tell her. "We have so many in the city. I loved to see them flying around the park."

"They build their nests under slides sometimes," she replies, nodding.

"And they're in basically every holiday story and song."

Dr. Luten cracks a serene smile. "That's true. My favorite is the one where they steal cakes and leave their footprints in powdered sugar all over the house."

"Well, we used to keep them as pets, right? With those claws and their brains, it was probably hard to keep them contained," I say, shuddering a little at the idea of trying to keep intelligent little creatures out of my sweets stash. It's hard enough to hide it from my mate, who barely even eats to begin with.

"Definitely. And that's part of the reason we stopped keeping them as pets. Collectively, I mean. Some people still do." She adjusts the collar of her white fur coat, her eyes drawn to the squabbling giants trying to negotiate with a massive Moon display determined to list to one side. "You can't actually *keep* pixies unless you want to lock them in a steel box. They keep themselves. Pixietamers have to convince a flight to stay, and if they choose to go..."

She shrugs. After another sip of her drink, she asks, "Do you know the origin of all those stories? The ones where pixies get into the feast before Moonrise?"

"Uh..." I wrack my mind, but nothing comes up. "No? I figured it was just a regular enough occurrence that everyone could relate. You know, since there's always so much food around at that time, and pixies were more common in homes."

"Well, that's true," she agreed, "but actually it's related to something a lot older than that."

Intrigued, I shift a little in my seat. It's not a large bench, so my attempt to get a more head-on look at her bumps my thigh into her hip.

It's not a hard hit, and I wouldn't think anything of it under normal circumstances, but I'm startled when a furious, high-pitched trill erupts from the furry depths of Dr. Luten's coat.

"Um—" I don't get a chance to ask her where it came from before the doctor continues, either oblivious or unconcerned.

"In many cultures, particularly in Eastern Europe, Scandinavia, parts of the Mongolian Steppe, and northern India, it was tradition to scatter flour or spices around offerings of food left out for pixies." She walks two fingers in the air to mime tiny little steps. "While the pixies ate the food, they'd walk in the dust. In the morning, people would find their tracks and interpret them to predict their fortunes for the year."

Briefly distracted from the sounds still coming from her coat,

I ask, “Wait, people actually left food out *for* pixies? I thought they were always stealing the Moonrise feast.”

“Well, it’s probably tied to that,” she replies. “I’ve seen some theories that folks put out offerings at first because they thought it’d distract the pixies from the real prizes, and the fortune-telling came later.”

“That makes sense, I guess.” I pause, waiting for her to address the squeaks and whistles coming from her coat. She doesn’t. “Might even be a fun tradition to bring back if people have a pixie problem.”

“Pixies aren’t a problem,” she asserts. “People are the problem. We bred them to live close to us and send our messages, but the moment we figured out a different system, we abandoned them. It’s not their fault. Yes, holes in walls obviously aren't ideal, but homes with a pixie population actually have dramatically fewer instances of pests because they eat insects and don’t tolerate rats or mice.”

The sounds coming from her coat appear to have multiplied. Setting my coffee on the arm of the bench, I abandon all pretense of politeness and gawk at her coat, which now appears to be moving.

Dr. Luten doesn’t seem bothered by it at all. She crosses one leg over her knee, her white boot bobbing up and down with an upbeat rhythm. “If everyone tried working *with* their pixies rather than trying to push them away, we’d all be better off,” she says, her calm voice a little firmer than before. Snorting, she jokes, “People might even be able to tell their future.”

I try not to notice, but it’s no use. I have to know. “Moira, I have to ask— What on Earth is happening in your coat?”

Looking a little surprised, like she can’t believe someone noticed the cacophony coming from her clothing, Dr. Luten pulls the collar from her neck.

Instantly, a little blue head the size of a pingpong ball erupts from the snowy fur.

I jump a little, taken aback by the dark compound eyes that fix on me. Tiny clawed fingers sink into the fur as it stretches upward, little nose twitching to get my scent. There's an iridescent gleam behind the creature — a flash of translucent wings.

A pixie stares me down, judging my worth, as Dr. Luten says, "This is Puck. I rescued him from a trap three years ago, but he couldn't be released because his leg was permanently damaged."

Still holding her collar away from her chest, she dips her chin to peer down into the depths of her coat. "And then he bonded with Crumble, and next thing I know they've started a flight."

Like they understood they'd been introduced, three more tiny heads pop out of the fur, all of them chittering and whistling. Little white fangs flash, showing off the weapons that catch the insects Dr. Luten talked about.

Astonished, I say, "You walk around with them?"

"Not all of them," she admits, stroking Puck's bald head with the tip of her finger. The pixie's compound eyes close in bliss. "Just the ones that volunteer. Puck's always game for a field trip, but the others don't always want to leave the nest."

Setting aside her drink, she digs in her pocket for a moment before she holds out a handful of tiny brown pellets. "Here," she urges, dumping them into my hand before I can object, "give them a treat. Who knows? Maybe they'll give you a fortune."

It's a little too late to object, and the gods know I've done crazier things, so I nervously hold out my handful of treats, palm up and fingers straight.

I expect the pixies to swarm, but they don't. Instead, they watch me closely, as if determining whether I'm worth accepting food from. I flounder for a moment, confused, before I default to the call every pet owner knows: kissy noises.

It's actually a relief when the swarm arrives. There's nothing worse than being rejected by an animal — except perhaps being rejected by an animal you thought was a pest half an hour ago.

A tiny cloud of blue explodes from Dr. Luten's coat. Wings buzz and teeth chatter as pixies hover around my hand, little fingers patting and grabbing. Before I know it, they're not just munching the pellets. They're climbing my arm, nibbling my fingers, and diving into my windbreaker. One even takes a shine to my ponytail and begins to swing from the end, a joyful whistle filling the air.

I'm laughing not just because of the absurdity — it's maybe the silliest interview I've ever conducted — but because it's also the cutest thing I've ever seen. I thought I knew pixies, but I'd never been so close to one before.

I certainly never had one nibble my cheek, its little blue hands patting and tickling as Dr. Luten explained, "They're grooming you. Well, Puck is. It means he likes you. And that you're maybe a little dirty. They're very fastidious little animals, you know. Super clean."

Closing one eye, I try to get control over my laughter enough to say, "Okay, rude, but I probably earned a little criticism. I had no idea you guys were so cute!"

"They are," Dr. Luten agrees, smiling as one of the smaller pixies zooms over to throw itself back into the warmth of her coat. Reaching inside to give it a stroke, she adds, "They're our friends. We just forgot."

Daring to give Puck a little tickle behind a large, batlike ear, I say, "Friends who can predict the future. You really are handy to have around, huh?"

Puck trills, one tiny hand sneaking behind *my* ear for a careful scratch. I smile, smitten, and think of the flour in my kitchen. I don't have a pixie problem at the moment, but I kind of wish I did.

Dr. Luten is the head of pixie research at San Francisco Protectorate University. She also runs a nonprofit pixie rescue called Forgotten Friends Rescue, which accepts donations. If you'd like to donate, know of a pixie in need of rescue, or learn more about how you can support your local pixie flights, she welcomes all inquiries.

Werewolves Have a Howling Good Time

Rasmus didn't like holidays, and contrary to popular belief, he wasn't much of a drinker. But he owned a bar, which meant all the sad fucks who had nowhere else to go on Moonrise came to him now.

Theoretically, he could've stayed home and crashed the pack's celebration, but he, like many of the bachelors in the new Merced Pack, couldn't stomach the lovey-dovey family shit. Being at The Broken Tooth was the best of two bad options.

Well, he thought, popping a chip into his mouth, *I suppose things could be worse.*

It wasn't like he was really *working.* He didn't do shit behind the bar. He'd inherited a damn good staff from the previous owner, which meant they were smart enough to keep him around only to sign the checks.

It was a pretty sweet gig. The gods knew he'd had worse jobs over the years. He'd grown up on the wolf pack's farm and he'd spent most of his formative years in one army or another, digging trenches and killing men. After that, it was all crime, scams, and scraping by.

Compared to all that, owning a bar in a city like San Francisco was living the high life. Of course, it helped that it gave him a clean transition into more legitimate business. Everyone needed a place to wash their money, and a bar was just below a strip club on that very particular scale.

What a bar had that strip clubs didn't, however, was social capital. Only a certain kind of person could be compelled to go into a titty zoo, but just about everyone could make up an excuse to dip into a dive bar. That made it a good meeting spot, and Rasmus was the man to make introductions.

That was a damn powerful position to be in. Favors and exchanges and secrets were a steady drip into his invisible coffers — not to mention his very real bank accounts.

But there wasn't much business to be had on Moonrise. The bar was lined with sad bodies stooped over half-finished drinks, and something about the attempt to liven up the place with cheap decorations actually made it more depressing.

Rasmus swept a judgmental gaze over the pathetic lot. At least his people didn't weep into their vodka. All the weres seemed to be having a damn good time as they bickered over a game of pool and tried to hustle each other. But weres had a lot of experience pushing aside piddling things like depression, loneliness, and dumb shit like missing family.

The first Moonrise after infection was always the hardest, but it got easier after that. Especially if one was lucky enough to find a pack.

None of the sad-sacks slumped against the bar had a pack. That much was obvious. A couple stray vampires sipped synth beside an arrant, and a smattering of other beings dotted the main floor of the bar. Most of them weren't talking. Their focus, weak as it was, tended to stay on the televisions mounted in corners playing an array of sports events. Only a lone screen behind the bar showed the annual bonfire lighting in the Orclind.

Rasmus looked away from the screen with a curl of his scarred lip. He'd spent too much time conscripted in the Orclind's army to ever be able to look at the territory the same. When he looked at those fields of bonfires and cheering crowds, all he saw were trenches and bodies.

He saw the green grass and the round stone homes and he thought of being dragged into a sterile cell. He felt the cold metal of his shackles. He remembered Josephine shivering, her delicate frame wracked by the chill, and how she tried to be kind to him.

And then he remembered the death of the only good part of him — and that pissed him the fuck off.

Suddenly realizing that he was dangerously close to becoming one of the pathetic lumps currently lining his cash register with their sorrows, he grabbed his basket of chips and hopped off the stool.

His fellow weres erupted into howls and cheers as someone, probably Woody, bagged a nasty shot. Rasmus normally liked the ruckus, but things grated at him a little worse this time of year. Feeling a headache building behind his left eye, he turned toward the poster-covered door to his office.

"Where're you going?" Orren, a big redhaired bastard who'd joined their pack shortly after Rasmus, called out. Pointing his pool cue toward Rasmus, he challenged, "You owe me a rematch for last time, when you *cheated.*"

Lifting one tattooed hand in a mocking wave, Rasmus replied, "Some of us have actual work to do. And don't blame me for your bad shot. It's not my fault you play like you've never met basic fuckin' physics before."

Orren blew a raspberry his way and showed off one clawed middle finger. "Sounds like you're running away to me!"

Scenting blood in the air, the rest of the weres joined in on the razzing. They stomped their feet, howled, and banged the ends of their pool cues on the table, all while demanding he face them for a game.

Normally he wouldn't put up with that kind of shit. His wolfish pride wouldn't let them think he'd been scared off from a challenge. Not to mention the fact that it was just some damn good fun. No one knew how to party like weres, because no one knew how important it was to take joy by the balls like they did.

But tonight he just couldn't.

Rasmus turned his back on the rowdy crew of ex-criminals, forgotten soldiers, and men with cosmically bad luck. Waving his hand over his shoulder in a dismissive gesture that morphed into an obscene one, he slipped into his office.

It wasn't nearly as nice as his office at home, but it was quiet. And quiet was what he needed.

Rasmus sank into the cheap rolling chair behind his cluttered desk with a heavy sigh. Dropping his basket of chips on top of a stack of papers that were probably important, he let his shoulders round.

He wanted to ignore the reason this year's holiday was worse for him than it had been for decades. He thought he'd gotten awfully good at ignoring the memories of his captivity and the torture he'd been put through while the good doctor celebrated the holiday with his wife and assistant.

Not Josephine, he recalled, protectiveness for the submissive still fresh and mean after so many years. *They treated her worse than a stray dog. Worse even than me.*

He wanted to ignore the memories of that brutal winter when he lost his soul more than anything, and usually he was pretty good at it. But when he stared at the open letter on his desk, he knew it was hopeless.

It was good, heavy cardstock he'd had to slice open with a clawtip. The invitation within was one of those fancy vellum-covered things with gold foil over the ritzy scrollwork. It looked like a wedding invitation, maybe, though he couldn't be too sure because he didn't get invited to those.

But it wasn't for a wedding. It wasn't even for a funeral, which would've been preferable.

It was for a gala celebrating the opening of an exhibit at the Fairmont, sent by the director personally.

Rasmus's throat constricted hard. His eyes smarted as he

stared at the stupid thing. *What a gift,* he inwardly snarled. *Can't we all just fuckin' move on?*

A roar of laughter from the bar made him blink and look away. Scarred lips tightening, he carelessly swiped it into a haphazard pile of bills and junk mail, revealing an official-looking letter from the city he'd been ignoring.

Figuring he was already in a sour mood, Rasmus tore into it with far less care than he had the invitation.

Finding only a letter from the sovereign's health board signed by Margot Goode herself notifying him and all relevant parties of new were-centered programs on the horizon, he rolled his eyes. They wanted his input and would he please, please contact the director of were outreach for a meeting? It was typical performative bullshit. The letter crumpled in his fist. Tossing it into the trash, he snatched another chip from the basket.

I may be a sad fuck, but I'm not a sucker. If they want to talk to me, they'll have to do it in person. He snorted, chip crunching between his molars with a viscous bite. *I'd like to see that director walk into this bar — but only if she's brave enough.*

The Amauri-Bowan Affair

For much of the world, the traditions of Burden's Moon revolved, in some abstract form or another, around surviving the brutality of winter and the depths of darkness.

For vampires, it was a time of freedom.

When the days shortened and night ruled, vampires were untethered by the sun's restrictions. Instead of bonfires and feasts — which they couldn't enjoy anyway — they threw monthlong parties, took extravagant vacations, went snow camping, or simply enjoyed the perks of being able to stay up far past their usual limits.

Dahlia didn't know what to make of it.

She understood that things would be different, and perhaps many of the traditions she'd grown up with wouldn't translate to her new existence. She'd gotten used to the wild parties that always hit The Lush like a tidal wave around the holiday, and that was certainly different than what she was used to.

But it was one thing to know it and quite another to experience it.

When she was used to breaking out the boxes of decorations and making plans with Cecilia for their annual Moonrise junk-food feast, all the Amauris around her were hopping on jets, planning ragers, or cramming as much into their social calendar as they could manage.

Prior to becoming a vampire, she never would've claimed to be a particularly devout worshipper of the gods, or even someone who *loved* the holiday. It hadn't exactly been a priority in her childhood home. But she'd come to love the traditions she shared with Cecilia, and it never occurred to her that someday she wouldn't be able to share those with a partner or their children.

It was a good thing, then, that she had Colin.

"I know what you mean," he said, poking at a crouton in his salad. "It was a hard adjustment for me, not doing those things with Alastair, but we both adapted eventually. And if I'm being honest, I've come to really enjoy not having *so* many family obligations around the holiday."

Dahlia pretended to sip from the synth she'd ordered. They both knew she wasn't drinking it, but it felt too awkward to sit there and watch someone eat without at least a beverage in hand.

"I don't want to force things on the Amauris," she admitted, "but I don't want to just abandon the parts of the holiday that mean something to me, either."

"And you shouldn't!" Colin waved his fork at her with enough gusto that a little splatter of salad dressing hit the white tablecloth. "Listen, these vampires are a loud, pushy bunch. They like getting their way, but the secret is they like pleasing us more. You've got to assert yourself and make sure they know what you need to be happy. If that's starting some new traditions around Burden's Moon, then so be it."

"What'd you do with Alastair?" she asked, fascinated by the idea of her adopted father getting exactly his way. It was hard to imagine him adapting to traditions he couldn't see the value in, or doing something silly like putting on a festive sweater.

Colin tipped his head from side to side as he chewed. His colored glasses slid a little on the bridge of his nose before he pushed them up with a knuckle. "Well, I tried a lot of different things over the years. For a long time, I forced him to go to at least one Moonrise or Moonset party, but it was such an obligation that eventually it sucked the fun out of it for me too. And you know, it didn't feel good, watching him not be able to really participate in the way I could."

Dahlia nodded. She wouldn't have liked that, either. Felix needed to be part of whatever she did, not slotted in as an afterthought. Ideally, *all* of the Amauris would be part of whatever she did.

"So what do you suggest?" she asked, rubbing the stem of her glass between her forefinger and thumb.

Colin shrugged. "Make new traditions. Take all the good things out of yours and the good things out of Felix's and mash them together like a festive baby."

"That's kind of what I was thinking," she said, eyebrows raising. "Actually, I had an idea."

"Go on."

Dahlia flattened both hands on the tabletop and leaned forward, as if she were about to impart a great secret she didn't want the restaurant to overhear. "I want *us* to do something. Throw a party, maybe."

He was quiet for a moment. "Us? As in your father and your anchor?"

"Yes," she answered, grimacing a little. "Do you think that's a terrible idea?"

To his credit, Colin didn't immediately balk. He also didn't exude enthusiasm, either. Instead, she got a perfectly reasonable noncommittal nod and headshake combination. "I don't think it's an *impossible* idea," he allowed.

"It wouldn't be a big one," she assured him. "Just the four of us. And maybe Tomas?"

"It's not impossible," he said again.

Dahlia licked her lips. "Right?"

"Right," he dragged out.

She pretended to sip her synth again to hide her grimace. *Not impossible. Sure. We'll see about that.*

It turned out to not be impossible at all. At least, logistically speaking. Anybody could plan a small family party, after all. The hard part was getting anyone to treat it like one.

Dahlia sat on the edge of the couch and glanced around the room with growing dismay. Felix lounged beside her, one ankle propped up on his knee, while her fathers sat on the couch opposite them. Tomas had occupied the chair by the fireplace, a glass of alcoholic synth in hand.

No one spoke.

Cheerful holiday music filled the air alongside the crackle of the fire. She'd commandeered an Amauri-owned penthouse above the glitter of downtown United Washington for their little get-together. Colin advised her that it would probably be a bit much to ask Alastair or Felix to enter each other's spaces, so she'd settled on a place that felt a little more neutral and spent a couple hours decorating it.

A sparkling garland of glass and silver beads had been draped over the fireplace mantle, and large pillar candles in cut crystal containers glowed on every flat surface. It felt strange only setting out a small platter of cheese, meats, and chocolate for Colin, but she channeled the energy she might've otherwise put into preparing food into more decorations, more candles, and more flowers.

Bouquets of white roses perfumed the air, and by the time she was done, she was proud to bits over the little winter wonderland she'd crafted.

And then the guests arrived. They'd barely managed the minimum of smalltalk before Felix and Alastair settled into a staring contest. Her husband smirked. Her father glared. The longer it went on like that, the worse the tension got.

Despite the pile of perfectly wrapped gifts on the coffee table and the festive music, it didn't feel much like a party. If anything, it felt like the start of a bad joke.

Four vampires and an arrant walk into a Burden's Moon party...

Dahlia sent Colin a pleading look. Sucking in a bracing breath, he summoned a wide smile and slung his arm around his vampire's shoulders. "So," he chirped, "this is nice, isn't it? Our daughter did such an incredible job with the decorations."

Alastair tapped his cane on the floor. Tilting his silver head slightly toward his anchor, he gruffly replied, "Of course she did. She's good at everything she does."

Dahlia flushed. "Not everything," she muttered, picking at the polish on her thumbnail.

One thing she didn't love about being a vampire was that her nails had gotten a lot thicker and sharper. The change made her a little self-conscious, which meant she'd also gotten *really* into manicures recently.

"That's the one thing we can agree on," Felix announced. Laying a hand on her wrist, he stalled her nervous picking. "Though I've got some complaints about her guest list."

Checking his phone, which had been vibrating off and on for the last few minutes, Tomas drawled, "I don't know. She got the ratio mostly right. Next time all she needs to do is leave the one Amauri in the room off the list."

Felix turned a sharp smile toward her cousin. Tapping the puncture wounds in his neck, he replied, "If you recall, there are *two* Amauris."

Alastair glowered. "Do *not—*"

"What? Complain about having to share air with the man who pointed a gun in my face and kidnapped my *bride?*" Felix's voice hardened in the way she knew meant he wasn't playing around or poking at the Bowans just for fun anymore. "Sorry, I don't forgive as easily as Dahlia."

Alastair bared his teeth. Shaking off Colin's hand, he leaned forward to remind her husband, "You kidnapped my *daughter*. You didn't even have the decency to bring her to her family before you sank your fangs into her. You didn't court her properly and you didn't show her an ounce of the fucking respect she's owed. I haven't even *begun* to forgive you, boy."

"Alastair," Colin warned, drawing him back into the cushions. "We talked about this."

Felix gave Alastair a disdainful look. "And you left her to bleed out on the rooftop, knowing full-well that there was a good chance she'd be turned. You *abandoned* your daughter, Bowan. You're fucking lucky she's deigned to have a relationship with you at all."

"There was no way for him to know his blood would take," Tomas snapped. "We'd never abandon our own. Unlike you family-killing degenerates."

"Hey!" she snapped, standing abruptly and cutting off what was likely the prelude of Felix pulling out the gun he thought she didn't know he'd brought. Sending a sweeping glare around the room, she reminded them, "This is my first Burden's Moon as a vampire and my first one without Cece in— in— since I was *five!* I cannot and I *will* not have my family fighting. Understood?"

Dahlia hadn't realized how upset she really was until she started talking. Humiliated by the way her chin had begun to wobble, she braced her hands on her hips and turned away from them all quickly.

"Aw, fuck," Felix breathed. The warmth of him radiated down her spine a moment before he wrapped his arms around her middle. "Don't cry, please. We'll stop fighting."

Colin hurried around the coffee table to stand in front of her. "We know how much this means to you," he assured her, wiping a tear from the corner of her eye with his knuckle. "No more fighting. Right, Alastair? *Tomas?*"

In a moment, she was surrounded by fretting vampires. Felix let them in close with hardly more than a growl, which she considered great progress.

Alastair smoothed a hand over her hair, ignoring the way her husband dragged her backward into his chest. "I apologize," he muttered, lips tight with displeasure.

Tomas didn't reach for her, which was probably smart. Instead, he fished for something in his pocket. Pulling out a key fob, he said, "We might not get along, but that doesn't mean we can't work together *sometimes.*"

Dahlia gave him an odd look as he dangled the key fob in front of her face. "What are you talking about?"

"This is the spare," Tomas informed her, a sly grin spreading across his handsome face. "You should probably beep it."

Felix skimmed his hands down her arms. Guiding her right hand away from her hip to accept the key fob, he nudged her toward the large windows that overlooked the street. "C'mon, pet. We started a group chat for this. You gotta make it worth the sacrifice."

Completely lost, Dahlia gave them all baffled looks as she slowly walked toward the windows. Squinting against the glare from the lights, she peered down at the street below and raised the key fob.

No sooner had her thumb hit the button than a flash of headlights lit up a dark corner of the street.

There, parked between two street lamps, was her car — or a new, redder version of the car Tomas had totalled.

Gasping, she cried, "My car! You got my— Wait, who's getting out of..."

Her heart stopped when a miniature pink-clad figure climbed out of the passenger's seat. She was too high up to see features clearly, but she didn't need to. She *knew* who that was in the same way she'd know the shape of her own reflection.

Felix's hand settled on the small of her back when she whispered, "Cece?"

Almost like she could hear Dahlia, the pink figure tilted her head up toward the penthouse. One tiny arm raised in a wildly enthusiastic wave as she jumped up and down, like she wanted to be absolutely certain she was seen.

Dahlia pressed herself against the glass, too astonished to do more than stare as her best friend grabbed the hand of a dark, helmeted figure that had slipped from the driver's seat. The two figures crossed the snowy street, clearly aiming for the building's entrance.

They were coming inside. They were *there.*

"Cece! Cece is here!" she cried, ripping herself away from the windows. Sprinting across the room in her sparkly stilettos and crystal-covered dress, she barreled past the grinning Bowans to get to the door.

She was so busy tearing toward the penthouse's entrance that she didn't pay any attention to the men who gathered in the sitting area.

Felix stood next to Alastair, hands tucked into his pockets and chin lifted with pride. "We did all right," he murmured, nudging Alastair with his elbow.

The older vampire sniffed. "You sure we can't convince her friend to move?"

"Nah," Felix replied, "but we can give Dahlia this."

Job done, Tomas tucked his phone away. "Whatever makes her happy."

Divya's Gift

The Lovers' Home was not so much an organization as it was a stepping stone. It was a place of charity, where those in need of an escape or a helping hand could receive meals, a safe place to sleep, and assistance.

But it wasn't just worshippers who benefitted from it.

When she chose to leave the Lovers' Refuge, where she'd been raised as a foundling and expected to take on the life of a priestess, it wasn't an option to simply walk out the door and into the real world. Not because it wasn't allowed but because the real world was an alien one.

She didn't know how to exist there.

Luckily, she wasn't the first foundling to leave the nest, as it were, and that meant there were systems in place to ease her transition.

The Lovers' Home had the structure she'd always known, but it was situated in the bright, pulsing heart of a city. She still served in the name of the goddesses, but she was paid for her work. She still lived among acolytes and a Head Priestess, but she could socialize outside of the confines of a Refuge's walls.

And beyond the Refuge's walls was... *everything.*

Divya marveled at the sight of Times Square decorated for the start of Burden's Moon. All around her, workers set up massive, glittering displays and towering screens flashed with color. Cars drove smoothly by on what she'd learned was an *m-grid* while people streamed over crosswalks.

She hadn't been raised completely ignorant of technology or media, but truly experiencing the energy of a city was incomparable to anything she could've imagined.

The sound, the scent, the *movement* — Divya felt as though she was standing in the eye of a storm. She hadn't decided if it was a storm she enjoyed yet, but if a lifetime of worship had taught her anything, it was to appreciate the majesty of the overwhelming.

And when she tilted her head back to behold the gleaming tower that dominated the skyline, she was certainly overwhelmed.

Truthfully, as much as she enjoyed the glitter of the holiday decorations and the rush of Times Square, neither were the reason she came there at least once a week.

Shielding her eyes from the glare, she held her breath and counted the winged figures silhouetted against the sky. Today there were four. There'd be more at lunchtime, when the Isand's staff took off from the roof, and again at dusk, when the business day ended. Occasionally she was lucky enough to catch them flying overhead at the Home, but it was a rare sight.

When the last dragon landed on the jutting platform at the top of the tower, Divya sighed and wandered in the direction of the Home. Tucking the sides of her white coat against her body, she traced a familiar path to the tiny cafe the acolytes had introduced her to.

She'd never had much of a fascination with dragons before, but she'd never known them as anything other than solemn worshippers. Now that she was in one of their capitals, she found their glamor and flashy colors as eye-catching as jewels.

Even the old couple who ran the Blue Flame Cafe were objects of quiet admiration. Both were variations of crimson that deepened into black at dusk, and when they stood together behind the counter, their tails twined in a sinuous display of affection. Divya loved to watch them, and she was infinitely grateful that they'd taken her under their wing, so to speak.

"Minu kingitus," Marika called out, "close the door! You'll catch your death if you stand in that cold any longer."

Divya hurried to do as she was told. The warmth of the cafe was almost oppressive compared to the frigid temperature outside. It seared her cheeks and the tip of her nose as she bypassed the handful of tables the cafe boasted in favor of the formica counter and vinyl-topped stools.

She came to the cafe whenever she had a free moment, and although they protested, she often found herself helping clean tables, organize condiments, and stack mugs behind the counter. Divya didn't know much about socializing or making conversation, but she could be useful.

It was lucky for her that Marika and Jaan didn't seem to mind her silent hovering or awkwardness. They'd "taken a shine to her," according to the High Priestess. It was hard to deny when they liked to drag her up to their roost for hearty dinners and kept trying to introduce her to their grandson, who'd recently been promoted to the Isand's Wing.

Not that she *would* deny it. Divya basked in their affection, and she thanked the goddesses at noon and midnight every day for their kindness.

"Good morning," she murmured, offering Marika a small smile. "Have things been busy?"

"Oh, always, always." Marika set a steaming mug of tea down in front of her without asking. Clicking her tongue, the old dragon eyed the thin coat Divya wore with clear disapproval. "What have you been doing, wandering the streets in that? It'll snow tonight! I woke up and smelled it in the air. Didn't I, Jaan? No, this won't do. You need a proper coat."

Divya gratefully accepted the tea. Wrapping her numb fingers around the warm ceramic, she said, "I'm used to snow. The Refuge was on a mountain, and this is the coat I wore there."

"No, no, not good enough! The ocean air is colder than

mountain air. Your skin is so fragile, and that coat looks old enough to be from my generation." Turning to holler through the square hole in the wall that opened up into the kitchen, she asked, "Jaan, where did I put our *kingitus's kingitus?*"

"In the drawer by the register, my Chosen," Jaan called back.

"Ah, that's right." Wings flexing, Markia bent at the waist with a grunt to retrieve a paper-wrapped package from beneath the counter.

Setting it in front of Divya, she explained, "I planned to wait until Moonrise, but I had a feeling you wouldn't have a proper coat, so... Go ahead, *kingitus.* Open it!"

"It's... for me?" She stared at the package with wide eyes.

Jaan's weathered face appeared in the hole in the wall. Bushy eyebrows raised, he rasped, "Who else would it be for? You act like you've never gotten a gift before!"

Divya flexed her fingers nervously around the mug. In a small, wavering voice, she admitted, "I haven't. We didn't give gifts in the Refuge. Charity was—"

"No gifts?" Marika's proud nose wrinkled. "Ridiculous! Open it now, *kingitus,* so you can start to catch up on everything you've missed!"

She stared at the package with a deep, painful sort of longing — and no small amount of guilt. "But I shouldn't..."

"You will!" Jaan crowed, pointing an arthritic claw in her direction. "Or we'll be offended!"

"We *will,*" Marika agreed.

"Oh." Divya flushed. Fingers uncurling from her mug, she delicately skimmed them over the shiny silver paper, feeling its creases and folds like she could memorize them.

There'd never been a *ban* on gifts, necessarily, but they also hadn't been done. The Refuge was a place of worship and service. For those raised there, things like individual wants and possessions just weren't considerations.

To have a *gift,* a thing purchased just for her by someone who had no reason to do so other than kindness... It was a different kind of overwhelming.

Divya bit her lip and gently slid her thumb under the paper's seam to tear the tape without harming the paper. She wanted to keep every part of the present, and she could already imagine what she'd do with the beautiful paper.

But all thoughts of crafts and keepsakes escaped her when she beheld the crimson coat hidden within the wrapping. Spreading it over the counter, she stared at the silver embroidery and tasseled belt with awe. It was heavy in her hands, far heavier than her thin white coat, and appeared to be handmade.

Divya had never seen anything so beautiful in her life.

Eyes stinging, she brought the coat to her face like it was her prayer cloth. Her first gift meant just as much to her as that cloth, which was the only thin connection to her mother she possessed.

"Thank you," she breathed.

A warm hand squeezed her shoulder. "You're welcome, *minu kingitus.* Now, let's see it on!"

Jaan smacked what sounded like a spoon against a pot. "Fashion show!"

Divya laughed, her tears soaking into the heavy wool. *Thank you,* she silently prayed. *Thank you, goddesses, for the gift of these people.*

The Holiday Black Market

The Market wasn't always about smuggling, shady deals, and cheap goods. During Burden's Moon, it also had some pretty great gifts.

The old soap factory was packed to the rafters with the usual suspects and those who came for the season. The grime and ramshackle stalls couldn't be disguised by fairy lights or garlands, but there was a certain magic to the atmosphere all the same.

Not to Olivier, of course, but he was fairly certain *someone* would appreciate it.

He wasn't there for the illegal goods or the Burden's Moon cheer. He was there for one reason and one reason only: his sister.

A few weeks prior, she'd taken him to see what had once been her underground clinic in this very Market. He'd asked her to, and despite her hesitation, she'd guided him through the massive fire code violation that was the soap factory. They'd been accompanied by her guard, of course, which meant they stood out like sore thumbs, but he didn't mind.

If people gave him a wide berth, all the better. And if people stayed far away from his delicate sister, it was safer for everyone involved — especially them.

The visit to her clinic, which she'd set up in secret to serve an overlooked community who otherwise might not have sought out a healer, was… enlightening.

And deeply distressing.

To know his talented, brilliant little sister had felt compelled to work in conditions like *that* made him sick to his stomach. He had no qualms with her providing services to the overlooked, but she had no reason to do it in a repurposed factory locker room, of all places. It didn't even have *heat.*

If he'd known, he would've had it renovated for her, top to bottom. No expense would be spared. No detail overlooked. If his sister wanted to save lives, then it was his honor to help her.

But he hadn't known. He hadn't known anything.

Olivier's jaw firmed as he pushed his way through the crowd. People did their best to step out of his way, but there wasn't much room for it. Hundreds of bodies crammed in the narrow alleys between stalls, filling the air with heat and competing scents. Even swathed in his thick black coat, gloves, and tinted sunglasses, his skin crawled with the sense of exposure that came with so many people so close to him.

But doing this for Margot was worth any amount of discomfort.

The stall she'd pointed out was close to her old clinic. Decked out in an atrocious amount of cheap Moon decorations and blasting festive music from a small speaker, the troll's electronics stand would've been hard to miss.

The man himself lounged behind the makeshift counter, phone in hand, and appeared to be completely uninterested in any potential customers that might want to purchase his dubiously supplied wares. It took Olivier a full minute to get his attention, and even that only came when he reached over the counter to silence the speaker.

"Excuse me," he drawled. "I'm looking for Jimmy."

"Found him," the troll grunted, barely looking up from his phone.

The man who ran the Market and who gave Margot the space

for her clinic was a mountain troll. His skin was a deep, dark gray and his body was as tall and thick as whatever mountain his people hailed from. Olivier imagined he was fairly good at intimidating people, which must've proved useful in his line of business.

Not that it worked on Olivier, of course, but he could imagine.

Narrowing his eyes at the troll, he announced, "A pleasure to meet you. I'm your new landlord."

Jimmy slowly lowered his phone. Arching his dark brows, the troll rumbled, "Wasn't aware the Market was for sale."

"It wasn't." Olivier offered him a cold smile. "I bought the building anyway. I'm good at things like that."

"And you are?" Jimmy eased out of his seat to stand with his arms crossed. "Besides a snooty elf with a stick up his ass, I mean."

"You don't need to know my name." Retrieving the pertinent papers from his pocket, Olivier pushed them across the counter. "All you need to know is that this is now my property."

The troll dragged the papers closer. Looking down at them, his expression gradually morphed from suspicious to outright incredulous. Eyes wide, he demanded, "What on— Why? What could an elf possibly want with this place?"

Olivier pushed his sunglasses up his nose with the tip of one gloved finger. "Only one thing."

"What?"

Tilting his head toward the clinic's closed door, he answered, "The clinic. I'm going to have it renovated and reopened with a dedicated healer. I don't care about rent. I don't care about what you do here. I only care about that clinic."

The troll looked lost. "But..."

"And," Olivier added with a grimace, "I want sprinklers installed. This place is a damn hazard."

Sweet Treats for Sweet Treats

"Isa!"

Artem pressed his phone to his ear as he ducked through the doors of the Draakonriik's embassy. "My sweet," he replied, nodding to the security personnel guarding the reception area. A smile tugged his lips at the sound of his daughter's clumsy fingers slipping on the cell phone. "Did you miss me already? I've only been gone an hour."

Emilia made the funny breathing sound all over-excited children seemed to make. "Um, I had a question."

Shocker.

His daughter was as intelligent as her mother, which meant there was hardly a minute of the day that went by without a question. Normally she peppered Paloma with them as they huddled up in her lab, all cozy in front of the monitors, but sometimes she liked to pick up the phone to ask her father something.

It seemed to be happening more often lately, but he couldn't complain. It was a privilege to be so loved by his child.

I can only hope I get as lucky with our second.

"You know I love when you call me, but I'm on my way into the office, my sweet," he warned her. "I have an important meeting in a few minutes. If your question is a quick one—"

"I *know* I'm not s'pposed to use the oven," she began in probably the most alarming way possible, "but if I wanna make a cake, how do I do that?"

Artem nearly stumbled in the hall outside his office. Sending a reassuring look to the staff who caught his odd movement, he ducked his head and hurried into his office. Speaking quickly, he demanded, "Is anything on fire, Emilia?"

"No," she drew out. "I didn't use the oven yet!"

A small sigh of relief escaped him. "Good. No ovens. Not after last time."

"I remembered!"

"I'm happy to hear it," he soothed. "If you want something, you should ask your mama. She'll help you when she has a moment."

"Mama's in bed," Emilia explained in that perfect little voice. "We were gonna make paper moons for the living room, but she doesn't feel good."

Artem winced. The urge to be back home in the nest, tending to his pregnant mate was a nearly insurmountable force inside him. Breathing deeply, he gently explained, "The baby makes your mama feel sick sometimes. She needs her rest, but—"

"If she throws up three times in a row, I'm s'pposed to call you," she finished for him. "I know, *Isa.* She only threw up once and then said she needed a nap."

Rubbing the back of his clammy neck, he sighed, "Okay, that's good. I'm sorry, sweet, but your mama can't give you cake right now. We need to take extra good care of her, and that means letting her rest."

"I don't *want* Mama to give me cake," Emilia huffed. "I wanna *make* Mama a cake!"

"What?"

"After she threw up, she said she shoulda had cake for breakfast instead of eggs. I checked the fridge but we don't have it." What sounded curiously like cabinets opening and closing came through the line. "I 'membered that Auntie Shiya taught me how to make a cake with flour and sugar and the oven, and then I 'membered that I'm not *allowed* to use the oven, and *then* I 'membered you said some things can be cooked in the microwave. Can you tell me how?"

Letting out an incredulous chuckle, he confirmed, "How to make a cake in the microwave for your mother?"

"Yeah!"

Artem's chest squeezed hard. "I'm sure your mama would love that, but how about I bring home a cake from the city? The bakeries are full of them for the holiday. We can share it when I come home. I'll only be a few hours."

Emilia paused. Speaking in a soft, confused voice that never failed to get her exactly what she wanted, she replied, "But... she threw up breakfast. She needs to eat now, *Isa.* What if the baby makes her sick again?"

Then I'll leave this damn meeting and fly home as fast as possible, he thought, rubbing his face. *Who cares about a Burden's Moon luncheon with the sovereign? I have better things to do.*

But in his heart, he knew that wasn't what Emilia really wanted. She was a giver, just as her mother and father were. Taking care of the people she loved was ingrained in her DNA. She didn't want him to rush home to solve the problem because she'd already figured it out.

And as they'd learned, allowing her to participate and help take care of Paloma helped her feel more in control of the uncertain situation that was preparing for a new sibling. If she could make her mother feel better, Emilia wouldn't worry quite so much, and that was more important than the state he'd find his beautiful kitchen in when he returned home.

"Okay," he said, crossing the room to deposit his briefcase on his desk. "I'm going to need you to get a piece of paper and a pen."

By the time he returned home, snow had begun to blanket the spiky tips of trees and the land around their roost. The sun hadn't set yet, but the sky was a deep, dark blue behind the thick clouds. A storm was brewing.

Like always, the scent of it in the frigid air brought back the best memories of his life.

He'd been saved by his Chosen in the winter, and they'd welcomed their daughter into the world in the middle of a snowstorm that kept them inside for days. All the best things in his life came on the heels of winter, and that didn't appear to be changing anytime soon.

His feet touched the platform for barely a moment before he hurried inside the atrium. "My sweets!" he called out, shaking the snow from his wings. "Where are my sweets?"

"Isa!"

Emilia's little red body came flying at him at lightspeed. She was just a streak of darkening crimson, knitwear, and little bluejeans as she careened around the corner to slam into his legs.

Sweeping her up into his arms, he pressed a dozen kisses to her cheeks — one for every time he thought of her during the day. "My sweet, I missed you! How did—"

Wiggling to be put down, she cried, "*Isa,* you need to try my cake!"

"Okay, okay," he laughed, "but I need to kiss your mama first!"

"She's in the kitchen," Emilia insisted. Tugging on his hand, she began to drag him with all the force her little body could manage.

Artem's brows furrowed. "Why is she in the kitchen?"

Paloma wasn't a bad cook, but in general she left those duties to him. The kitchen was his domain in the same way that the lab was hers. It was his pleasure to cook for his family, especially when she was busy growing a child in her body and making scientific breakthroughs at the same time.

"She was helping me clean," Emilia explained. It turned out not to be necessary, since he had two eyes that were perfectly capable of seeing what had been done in his kitchen.

He stopped in the entrance, mouth agape, to stare at his grinning Chosen. She stood by the sink, a sponge in hand. All around her was... chaos.

Flour, every measuring cup they owned, half the spice cabinet, and approximately twelve mixing bowls were scattered around the room. Nearly every surface was either sticky or powdered, and it looked like the inside of the microwave had been used as the container for a catastrophic experiment.

Snickering at his expression, Paloma set her sponge aside. "We wanted to clean up before you got home!"

"I... left early," he wheezed. Clearing his throat, he forced himself to step inside the destroyed room to sweep his Chosen into his wings. Lowering his head so he could whisper in her ear, he asked, "How are you feeling?"

Pressing a kiss to his cheek, she answered, "A ginger ale and some saltines fixed me right up. I'm fine."

"Good," he sighed. "But what happened here? This isn't all from a cake, is it?"

"She said you told her how to make it," Paloma whispered back, obviously delighted.

"I didn't tell her to set a bomb off in the kitchen!"

Paloma tenderly tucked a lock of hair behind his ear. "Oh, you've done worse. Remember when you tried making candy?"

Before he could argue that he'd *never* done anything on the level of pure devastation that had visited his favorite room in the house — besides their nest, of course — Emilia tugged on his pant leg.

"We saved you a slice!" she chirped, as proud as he'd ever seen her.

Artem reached for the plate a half a second before his brain caught up with his eyes. "Ah," he choked, tentatively accepting her offering. "My sweet, why is it *green?*"

"She added food coloring," Paloma solemnly explained. "It was a masterful artistic choice to fit the holiday."

He held the plate up to his face for closer inspection. A tiny, nearly flat slice of what looked more like a sickly green pancake sat in the center. A heap of powdered sugar had been piled on top in lieu of icing, and when he gave it a sniff, the scent of cinnamon was so strong he had to fight back a sneeze.

Glancing at his Chosen, he found her watching him with her lips rolled between her teeth and her eyes sparkling. He knew that look well. It meant he was in for trouble.

Summoning a wide, impressed smile, he turned to his daughter. "It looks incredible!"

"Try it!" she demanded, hopping from little red foot to little red foot. "You need to try it!"

Bracing himself, he lifted the wet, spongy triangle from the plate.

The texture hit him first. Then it was the spice.

Artem struggled to get it down, but he'd be damned if he let it show on his face — even *if* his Chosen was quietly laughing at him.

"S'delicious," he mumbled.

"I'm gonna bring it to the Moonset potluck," Emilia exclaimed, chest puffing.

"O-oh," he choked, trying to ignore the way Paloma had hurriedly turned around to face the sink. Of course, he could still see her shoulders shaking, which really negated the gesture.

Setting the rest of the uneaten slice on his plate, Artem sank onto his knee to pull Emilia in for a hug. He had to clear his throat first, but he managed to rasp out, "I think that's a great idea. How about we do it together next time?"

"Okay," she replied, "but Mama gets the first slice!"

"Of course she does," he agreed, sending his grinning Chosen a look that promised retribution. "My sweet treat gets first dibs on all sweet treats. *Especially* the green ones."

Tank's Worst Gift Ever

There were a lot of reasons to spend Burden's Moon alone. Contrary to popular belief and what the media's holiday industrial complex liked to push, it wasn't an inherently magical time of year or a mandatory activity.

For people like Tank, it was best avoided at all costs.

He'd seen enough fires when he fought on the front lines, and all the noise and singing and fireworks were a sensory nightmare for a man like him. Not to mention the pressure that came with gift-giving, as well as the pity invites to feasts from well-meaning folks who knew a little too much about his situation.

So he didn't have a clan. Big whoop. It was more convenient than anything else. He didn't have anyone to make excuses to every year.

He could do exactly as he liked, which was usually working in his garage until the sound of fireworks became too much. Then he'd shotgun half a bottle of whiskey, put his ear plugs in, and pass out in his nest until noon the next day.

So far, things were going exactly to plan.

Rock music thumped from the speakers in his garage, drowning out most of the noise of his small town's celebrations, as he lay on his back beneath his neighbor's truck. The roller's wheels squeaked as he pushed himself a few inches, trying to get a better angle on a stubborn bolt.

"Fuck me, Tim, when was the last time you changed the oil on this thing?" he muttered.

It was a common misconception that ranchers and farmers took better care of their vehicles than city folk. The truth was that they knew just enough to run the poor mechanical beasts into the ground. Tank hadn't been out of work for more than a day at a time in Montague since he set up shop.

There was always a tractor on its last legs that needed services *right just now* or a truck that'd somehow managed to run with its engine block held together by shoelaces and duct tape. Unlike in the city, his services were *always* in demand.

Tim wasn't the worst offender in town. In fact, he normally did his damndest to avoid bringing his trucks in for servicing because he thought he was a pretty decent self-trained mechanic. But he'd noticed the truck making the oddest noise that morning and couldn't seem to diagnose the issue no matter how hard he tried, so the gift of a Burden's Moon distraction had been delivered to Tank's garage just in time.

The roller squeaked again as Tank struggled to get the bolt to move. Gritting his teeth, he tried putting some real muscle behind it. Planting his boots firmly on the concrete floor and quickly locking the roller's wheels, he yanked hard.

The roller squeaked again, louder this time, just when the bolt finally began to give. Except he hadn't moved. His feet were firmly fixed to the ground and the roller was locked.

Tank froze.

Below the thumping music and the sporadic, hair-raising blasts of fireworks outside, there was nothing.

Then, almost too faint to be heard, there was another squeak.

"Aw, fuck," he sighed, dropping his wrench. Rubbing his eyes with one grimy hand, he listened to yet another squeak that sounded suspiciously like a meow.

You tell people to check their fuckin' cars during the winter and they never do, he silently grumbled. He'd lost track of the number of cats, squirrels, birds, and even racoons he'd pulled out of engines and wheel wells. He'd certainly done enough to recognise the sound of a kitten when he heard one.

It took the better part of two hours and a stiff drink later, but eventually he spied the big yellow eyes of a kitten lost amongst the tubes and valves of a greasy engine. "All right," he growled, shoving his hand down into the toasty little hole the feline had taken refuge in. "You don't belong there. You want to get burned up or something? You do that and *I'll* be the one scraping your toasted fur out."

Tiny claws and even smaller fangs gave a good fight, but they were no match for his orcish hand. Pinching the scruff of the kitten's neck, Tank hoisted the stowaway out with as much care as he could under the circumstances.

No bigger than the size of his palm, with a grease-smeared white coat and one brown patch over its right eye, the thing couldn't have been cuter if it tried. And it *didn't.*

A mighty hiss curled its whole tiny body and showed off pale pink gums as it attempted to assert its dominance over the orc holding it captive.

"Don't give me that," Tank growled. "I saved your ass. Do you know what could've—"

An explosion rattled the garage as another firework, this one far bigger than the others, lit up the sky over his home. Tank flinched and swore, his heart pounding as old instincts screamed.

Dangling from his hand, the kitten curled into a tight ball and stared at him with wide, panicked eyes.

"You don't like 'em either, do you?" Tank shook his head and drew the kitten close to his chest. Baby claws sank into his shirt and pricked his skin, but it didn't hurt much. If anything, the tiny bit of discomfort helped ground him as he stomped away from the partially disassembled trunk.

When another firework screamed through the air, he cupped

the shivering kitten's back and hurried into the house. "It'll be better in here," he promised them both.

It was certainly warmer, and the fireworks weren't quite so loud in the semi-underground structure of his homestead. Hands shaking, he found himself compulsively petting the feral little grease ball who clung to him.

Can't leave him all covered in oil, Tank thought. *No one will take him if he's dirty.*

And since *he* certainly didn't want a cat, he figured he ought to give the kitten a little bit of a spit shine. He'd call around to see if anyone needed a mouser in the morning, he decided, heading for the kitchen sink.

Tank expected more hissing and biting as he lowered the kitten into a soapy bath of warm water, but that's not what he got. Perhaps the fireworks had put the fear of Loft in him, or maybe he'd just run out of steam. Either way, the kitten stared up at Tank with the saddest golden eyes as the orc clumsily scrubbed dish soap into his fur.

Pitiful complaints rose from the soaked kitten, tugging at long-disused heartstrings. "I know," Tank muttered. "It's almost over. How's about a can of tuna after this, huh?"

The kitten had no idea what he said, obviously, but it didn't seem to matter. As soon as Tank got him thoroughly rinsed and wrapped in a kitchen towel, the little creature began purring like a finely-tuned engine.

Setting the kitten in front of the cast iron fireplace with an open can of tuna, as promised, Tank eased into his favorite seat with a sigh. He'd fetched himself a drink, too, but he barely touched it as he watched the damp kitten attempt to eat too-big mouthfuls of tuna and purr at the same time.

Worried that the kitten would eat himself sick, Tank made an executive decision and removed the can when he'd finished half. This was met with loud complaints, but the kitten must not have been too upset because the moment Tank retook his seat, the cat sprang onto the couch and clawed his way onto the orc's shoulder.

"That's all right, I guess," he mumbled, scratching the cat behind one triangle-shaped ear. "S'long as you don't think you're staying, you know. I'm not a cat person."

A rattling purr and the press of a cold nose on his neck was his only response. Tank sighed and leaned into the cushions, his claws idling sifting through drying fur. His drink sat forgotten on the side table as he said, "Guess you should have a name. Might take a while to find someone to take a baby mouser, and I can't just call you cat."

Thumbing one silken ear, he offered, "How's Grease? You know, for that spot you've got."

The cat didn't reply. Those harmless little claws began to knead Tank's shoulder, though, which he took as a positive sign. "That's settled, then," he announced, lifting up the collar of his flannel to tuck around the little furball. "But you're not staying, remember? Don't get too comfortable."

Despite the noise outside and the memories that threatened to grip him by the throat, Tank found his eyelids lowering as he made himself comfortable on the couch. Eventually, he settled on it long-ways, his boots discarded, and Grease curled up on his chest. He never seemed to stop purring, and Tank never seemed to stop petting, and before they both knew it, they were asleep.

Well… maybe I could use a mouser, Tank thought, drifting off.

A Cold Diamond

Roxelana Zorya didn't know what other families did for the holiday, but hers threw a party. Not the kind she'd read about in books and seen in films, with warm smiles and comfortable sweaters and baked goods.

Her family's tradition was... colder.

She observed the soiree with tired eyes. In her gloved hand, champagne bubbled in a crystal flute. It was still full. Her aunt and uncle were busy discussing important things across the ballroom, but that didn't mean she was unobserved. If her aunt caught her sipping alcohol, she'd never hear the end of it.

It was bad form to *not* have a drink in her hand, but it was even worse to risk getting drunk around influential company.

And her aunt and uncle didn't keep any other type of company.

Being related to one of the Five Families meant they held a certain sway, and being one of the families that firmly believed in keeping the old order of things meant they only associated with elves like them.

Roxelana hated it. *All* of it.

She hated being locked in the house. She hated the idea of being forced into a loveless union. She hated the fawning and the snide comments and the sheer, unearned audacity of every single self-important asshole in the room.

When an elderly woman she knew had an unbetrothed son made eye contact with her, she quickly pretended to hear her name across the ballroom. Her silk gown — bias-cut and a perfect shade of cream to complement her blue skin — brushed her ankles as she did her best to hurry without looking like she was doing exactly that.

People murmured at her as she passed beneath the massive crystal chandelier, offering platitudes and well-wishes they didn't mean. She gave them all practiced smiles but didn't stop. If she slowed down, someone would catch her, and then there'd be no extracting her from the uncomfortable conversations her family's allies wanted to have.

The parties had never been comfortable before, but turning thirty had made them far, far worse. Thirty was when she legally assumed her position as heir, and when she was eligible for a union with any of the scions of the assembled families — which she had absolutely zero interest in.

The more people tried to catch her attention, their eagerness to attach themselves to the sole heir of Zorya family giving them a mad, slack-jawed sort of look, the worse the sense of suffocation became. The weight of the glittering diamond collar around her neck got heavier and heavier, until she imagined she could feel it cutting into her flesh to draw that precious green blood from her veins.

None of these people, her aunt and uncle included, cared about her. They didn't even care about the holiday. They cared about using her, and they cared about having an excuse to show off their wealth — which didn't hold a candle to the inheritance her parents left her. The fact that throwing this party put her on display like a piece of meat up for sale was an added benefit.

They'd been waiting for the moment they could sell her off in a union for most of her life. Doing so would not only buy them powerful allies in the traditionalist circles they ran in, but it would also entitle them to a significant pay-out from her parents' will.

And that wasn't something they would risk twice.

She didn't have a specific goal when she crossed the ballroom. Only the overwhelming desire to get away, to get as far from every single one of these elves as possible propelled her toward the exit. Instinct clawed at her, demanding she run as fast as her heels could take her.

Glancing over her shoulder, she spied her aunt and uncle with their heads bent together. They were whispering with one of the top contenders for her union contract. If nothing else made her want to run, it was *that.*

Roxelana slipped out the door that led to the sprawling garden. Her breath exploded out of her in quick, desperate puffs of fog as the cold hit her. Portland glittered below her, dusted in a light snow, and the manicured gardens of her family's home stretched out beyond the patio.

Abandoning her champagne on the stone patio railing, she quickly descended the steps into the garden. It was unlikely someone would follow her. It seemed that she was the only elf in the world who actually enjoyed being out in nature, so none of her would-be suitors would be inclined to accompany her.

And it wasn't like her aunt and uncle were worried about her running away. They'd made sure that was impossible.

The diamond choker heated against her neck the farther she got from the main house. Soon enough it would start to vibrate, and then... Well, she'd only tested that once before, and it'd been agonizing enough to keep her in line ever since.

Roxelana's heels sunk into the fine gravel of the garden path with every step, but she didn't let it stop her. Snow settled on her silvery hair and bare shoulders as she sought out her favorite spot in the garden.

Hidden below the wispy boughs of a stooped and bare willow was a small, icy pond. And tucked beside them both was a wrought iron bench she'd spent nearly every afternoon of her life reading on.

Ignoring the snow, she sank onto the bench with a weary sigh. Her gloved fingers curled around the edge of the seat as her shoulders slumped and her head bowed. The weight of what was possibly happening in that ballroom without her input, let alone consent, made her feel... old.

Old and tired and so, so sad.

She'd never had a lot of hope before. It wasn't like her fate was a surprise. Her aunt and uncle had been upfront with her about their plans from the moment they took custody of her. But it all seemed so much easier to deal with when she didn't have that single, shining moment of *life* to cling to.

Her first trip to the capital. Her first exposure to the outside world. Her first introduction to Others.

Her *only*. Her *last*.

All outside privileges had been revoked. She'd become a flight risk. For five years, her world had been nothing but denied instinct and the threat of a looming union she couldn't stomach.

"I don't regret it," she whispered to him, as she often did when she sat on the bench. "If all I got was a moment, I'm still grateful for it."

Roxelana leaned back against the cold iron to stare up at the sky. A heavy moon glowed through the clouds, illuminating the fluffy snowflakes that spiralled down to kiss her cheeks. She imagined what it would be like to soar through those clouds.

No family to chain her. No choker to keep her prisoner. No fear or sadness.

If she had wings, she could find him.

But she didn't. In this life, she had more money than the gods and a future of misery planned out for her down to the last detail.

Closing her eyes, she imagined the consort she'd only known for a moment. "May you find warmth on the darkest night," she whispered. "Because I won't."

Frozen Worlds

It's a rare thing, to find darkness unoccupied.

On land, shadows writhed with the dead and reborn. In the air, a flash of wing was all prey might see against the twinkle of a star before the end came. And in the water, merfolk claimed the dark.

They weren't constrained to the oceans, either.

Carried by the tectonic forces of glaciers and earth-splitting rivers, they found their way into the deep waters of the world. Some traveled to and from the ocean, traversing deltas and streams with the season. And some, like the Lake Tahoe pod, had thrived in isolation for hundreds of generations.

High in the Sierra Nevada mountains, Lake Tahoe was a world unto itself. Frigid, crystal clear waters spanned one hundred and ninety-one square miles, and every one of them was claimed by an unbroken chain of merfolk.

Rarely seen by the scattered resort towns and ski lodges that clung to their home's edge, the merfolk had little interest in the outside world. They showed themselves for three reasons and three reasons only: to trade, to mate, and to worship.

On the darkest night of the year, when the snow fell and the edges of the lake became shattered glass, their dark bodies rose from the darkest depths to greet the sky.

Those that dared live in the towns during the winter gathered on docks and along the shoreline to exchange offerings. Handmade gifts, food, and trinkets left and entered webbed hands with murmured well-wishes. Children, merfolk and land-dweller, chattered as adults caught up.

Many of them had done the ritual with the same groups all their lives, creating a tapestry of connections that spanned generations. The darkest night was lit with bonfires, flashlights, and the joy of reuniting with friends.

The differences that separated them fell away, and if one was lucky, a new connection might be made under the cover of darkness — a gift all its own.

The Orclind's Biggest Party

It was supposed to be the party of a lifetime. That's what he'd been told. That's what everyone said.

Go to Boulder, people told him. *The Moonset festival is the biggest party in the UTA!*

But no one fucking told him that you could get altitude sickness by just being in the damn place.

Crash groaned. The cool tile of the hotel bathroom helped soothe a little bit of his discomfort, but not much. The nausea was like a wet blanket draped over his whole body, pressing him down into the floor and leaving him kinda damp all over.

Outside, the sounds of fireworks and pounding music heralded the festivities he couldn't attend. Thousands of people from all over the world were gathered in the streets, drinking, eating, and hunting for someone or some*ones* to spend the night with. He'd had so many grand plans to be among them.

Every single one was shot straight to Grim's riverbank when he woke up that morning in a cold sweat, unable to catch his breath and about two seconds from chucking his guts into the toilet.

"Seemed like such a good idea," he whimpered to no one. "Why did this seem like a good idea?"

Because Cece talked about it.

Crash pressed his face into a rough hotel towel, half-hoping he could smother himself into passing out and forgetting all about his ex.

It didn't work. Not much did, besides getting absolutely obliterated or finding someone to bash him over the head with a pipe.

Cece was just one of those girls a man didn't forget.

He wasn't surprised when she broke it off with him. He'd known from the moment they met that she was too damn good for a piece of shit like him. Smart, funny as shit, more confident than a vampire at midnight, and so beautiful it hurt to look at her, Cecilia Warren was a taste of the good life he didn't deserve.

They'd had fun together, sure. He'd tried to treat her right, in all the ways a rough-edged orc who didn't always fall on the right side of the law knew how, but in the end, they both knew it wouldn't last.

She wasn't his mate. He wasn't a good fit for a ray of sunshine with a good life ahead of her.

But he was still fucking sad, and he fucking hated being fucking sad, so he bought a stupidly expensive last-minute ticket on an m-jet to Boulder, grabbed his bag, and set off to lose himself in alcohol for at least twenty-four hours. Cecilia had mentioned to him once that she wanted to go to the legendary festival, so he supposed it'd been lodged in his head and came up again as some pathetic way to reconnect with her — kinda like a parasite or one of those tumors with teeth.

It figured that it was a disaster.

The universe didn't want them together. It didn't even want him thinking about her, apparently, because it'd struck him down with the most pathetic sickness he could imagine.

"I'm an *orc,*" he whined into the towel. "We're built for mountains, for fuck's sake!"

As if on cue, the universe responded with its own *fuck you* in the form of a disrespectfully loud pop and shatter of fireworks over the hotel.

A shudder wracked him as another wave of nausea crested. Pushing himself onto his hands, he pulled himself across the tile like a sweaty green seal. Crash slung his muscular body over the bowl of the toilet and hung his head, waiting for the inevitable.

When the deed was done, he thought, *Well, I guess this could've been worse. If Cece was here, I'd be humiliated. What woman wants an orc who can't handle a little altitude?*

A hoarse laugh escaped his scorched throat as yet another round of fireworks seemed to indicate the universe agreed with him. Heartbreak sucked, but at least he had his pride. Or what was left of it, anyway.

"Aw, fuck." He staggered upright to rinse his mouth. Stumbling back into the main room, he collapsed into bed.

Crash groped mindlessly for his phone, hidden somewhere in the sweaty knot of blankets, as the colorful lights from the fireworks shone through his window. Squinting at the screen, he pulled up the airline's app to change his ticket.

He should've never come, and he didn't intend to spend another hour in the wretched city if he didn't have to. He wanted his own damn bed in his own damn apartment in his own damn city, where he didn't feel like his brain was being squeezed in a vice and memories of his ex came up as regularly as vomit.

Heartbreak, it turned out, couldn't be fixed with a party. Even if the party was legendary.

Sugar and Snow

It was Burden's Moon, a time for peace and clan, when he spotted her from across the battlefield approximately three seconds before a grenade blew up in his face.

It wasn't the first time it'd happened to Henrik. After seventy years on the Orclind's front lines, he'd been blown up, sliced, shot, and beaten in just about every way a person could imagine and most ways they couldn't. A grenade didn't faze him much.

And it sure didn't knock the sight of her out of his head. Although he did question whether she was real or not for a moment, because that sort of thing had happened to him once or twice.

Henrik pushed himself out of the blood-soaked mud and grit, his ears ringing, and tried to focus his doubled vision on the woman in white. They'd ambushed the shifter battalion just before sunrise, sending the camp into bloody chaos as men ran for their guns and animals exploded from skin.

It was a large camp meant to act as a command center for several other smaller units, which made it a juicy target for an orcish raiding party like Henrik's. Not only could they loot the supplies sitting nice and pretty in crates, but they could take men out when they thought they were safe surrounded by so many others.

It made sense that they'd have a healer — or it did once, back when the war was still new. Henrik couldn't remember the last time he'd seen one on the battlefield. He'd even heard whispers among his men that they were all dead.

That was how they knew the world was coming to an end. When there were no more healers, the gods would abandon them — if they hadn't already.

His stomach lurched as he focused his swimming vision on the white figure knelt in the mud several yards away from him. For a moment, she didn't look human. She looked like Grim herself, dressed all in white, come to bring mercy to the wretched souls caught in the war.

Snow had begun to fall, veiling her in a pale glow. It softened the world between bomb blasts. Even from several yards away, he could make out the way snowflakes settled on her, as soft and gentle as a touch from the goddess she so resembled.

Mercy, he thought, something in him moving with tectonic force. The goddess of death and mercy knelt before him, wreathed in pure white snow, and whispered in his ear again, *"Mercy."*

And then she twisted her upper body, turning to face him as she tried to save her patient. A flash of red broke the illusion of divinity and brought her back to the battlefield.

Her apron was soaked with blood, nearly obscuring the Healer's Hand emblazoned on her chest.

That symbol should've protected her. It should've protected all the healers, no matter what side of the war they fell on, but it'd become a target instead. Everyone knew that the quickest way to knock out a battalion was to take out their healer, and as the war dragged on, their numbers dwindled.

Officially, their orders were to capture any healers found in battle and conscript them into service, but in the heat of a firefight, the chances of being able to do that successfully were low.

And if capture wasn't an option...

"Healer!" someone to Henrik's left bellowed. His head swivelled just in time to see a rifle lift.

Instinct roared in furious denial. He'd seen too many innocent healers murdered, and this one could not, *would* not join their numbers.

Without thinking, he sprang to his feet. His hammer, a bloodied weapon that'd seen more battles than it should've, swung in a wide arc through the smoky air. The impossibly heavy weapon slammed into his fellow soldier with a sickening crunch. The rifle flew out of the orc's hand and landed in the snow-topped muck that'd once been a field.

Henrik didn't wait for the soldier to hit the ground before he swung the hammer back toward his side and tucked it close, making running easier. His vision still wasn't quite right, but it didn't stop him from sprinting toward the healer.

Bullets whizzed by his ears as he made his huge body a target for every shifter on the battlefield. Several grazed him, but none managed to stop him. His hammer was a heavy weight in one hand as his boots sank into the churned soil, made thick and sticky by slush and freshly spilled viscera.

Despite the dust and smoke and snow in the air, his vision narrowed to that slim white figure knelt in the filth like a glowing beacon. He saw and heard nothing around him even as he swept aside a rugged, blond-haired shifter with a vicious blow of his hammer. The bite of bullets didn't slow him down, and neither did the percussive blasts of explosives pockmarking the landscape in all directions.

For as long as he lived, Henrik would never forget the moment she looked up at him.

Mercy.

The war disappeared. The blood, the pain, the misery of decades of fighting for nothing — all of it vanished when she finally looked up from her work to see the storm bearing down on her.

Large eyes set in a moon-shaped face met his own with neither fear nor resignation. She stared him down, her chin set and her hands still pressed into the flesh of her mangled patient.

She didn't try to run. She didn't flinch or scream.

The healer watched a battle-hardened orc carrying a bloodied warhammer come down on her without a modicum of fear.

In another life, at another time, he might've stumbled. He might've lost his mind completely as he beheld the perfect creature staring back at him like a goddess come down to ease the suffering of mortals.

But in this lifetime he was a soldier, and when a cry of warning went up, he didn't stop to think about anything besides keeping her alive.

It was pure instinct to fling his body over hers a mere moment before an explosive detonated only a few feet away.

He landed hard on top of her, his much larger and tougher body pressing her into the filth. The shifter she'd been tending to didn't even have a moment to let out a cry before his battle was ended, taking him far beyond what even the best healers could do. Heat flashed across Henrik's body, searing him through the layers of his thick wool uniform and armor.

The pain barely registered.

The world went very still as he pressed his face into the healer's dark hair, revealed by her fallen hair-covering. Despite the acrid smoke and blood that permeated everyone and everything on the battlefield, the scent of violets reached him.

Another flash of heat, so very different from that of an explosive, scorched the flesh of his hands and feet.

Henrik gasped, his powerful limbs contracting around the soft body below him. Something inside him cracked open under the force of an invisible hammer's blow, letting loose a flood of instinct.

My mate. My mercy. My blessing.

The words were formless but certain, an unshakeable feeling that brooked no argument. They came from something inside of him that was beyond logic, beyond battlefields or loyalty to clan and queen. They were immutable and undeniable.

Henrik rose up on his hands to behold the blessing he'd been given. She lay beneath him, her eyes closed but her breathing steady, apparently knocked unconscious either by his hard landing or the explosive.

Raising a shaking hand, he cupped her dirtied cheek. His flesh, once a pale gray, had blackened not from the dirt, but from the gift he never dreamed he'd receive: the kohl.

"Thank you," he breathed, stroking the smooth skin below the grime. His voice was little more than a smoke-roughened croak. Even if she'd been awake to hear it, she might not have understood it.

The cold mud shuddered under them as another bomb went off. Debris flew over their heads, pelting his back with stones, bits of what was once an encampment, and the gods only knew what became of men when they met explosives.

Instinct had always been a powerful force in him, but he'd never experienced it like he did then.

Henrik's vision sharpened as a wave of adrenaline washed over him. He didn't feel his wounds or his fatigue. There was no hunger or the persistent soreness of a body that'd seen too much battle.

He was *new*.

All at once, he understood what he had to do. Henrik didn't have time to be gentle as he slung his mate over his shoulder. She weighed less than his field pack, which he'd somehow managed to retain through the ambush. Gripping the backs of her thighs with one possessive hand, he held tight to his hammer and surged to his feet.

"All will be well," he promised his healer. Fear and worry evaporated. All that existed in him was the instinct to protect her and the unshakeable certainty that he'd do anything to earn the gift the gods had given him — even if that meant abandoning the cause he'd sacrificed seventy years for.

No, he thought, eyeing the horizon through the smoke. *I didn't fight for the Orclind.*

Seeing a narrow opening in the fighting, he bent at the waist and charged. His boots threatened to slide in the slushy mud, but he somehow managed to keep his balance as he dodged snarling shifters and the ear-shattering pop of explosives. His own people didn't fire on him, though they should have. If they noticed he was running *away* from them rather than toward them, they did so far too late.

His legs never carried him faster than they did when he sprinted with reckless speed through the battle.

When he finally cleared the smoke, he didn't stop.

When the sounds of gunshots and bombs exploding faded, he didn't stop.

When gentle snow became a howling blizzard, he didn't stop.

He ran until he could run no more, compelled by the ancient instinct to protect and hide that which was most precious. He ran and ran, blood soaking his uniform and fingers gone numb from cold.

Only when he reached the remains of an abandoned town did he finally slow.

I did it for her, he realized, nearly delirious with exertion and blood loss. *I did all of this for her. Now I have to get her safe. She needs a nest. Where can we nest?*

The sky was rapidly darkening. The cold was as sharp and clean as a blade on his tongue. The building storm added to the pounding urgency in his veins. He could survive the elements, but his fragile mate couldn't.

It was another blessing that found him stumbling blindly into the nearly collapsed shell of a factory. Barely visible on a scorched brick wall were the words *Western Beetsugar*.

All in all, it looked entirely unfit for habitation from the outside, which was probably why it'd been overlooked by scavengers and others seeking shelter. When Henrik took his hammer to a heavy metal door on the undamaged side of the building, he was astonished to find a nearly untouched office.

It appeared that the main manufacturing zone had been the hardest hit, but the administrative center had been untouched — including what he could only assume was the boss's office.

As the wind began to howl outside, he deposited his mate onto the tile floor as gently as he could. Henrik resealed the metal door and barricaded it with several heavy desks before he prowled around the rooms, hammer in hand. When no threats appeared and now armed with the knowledge that a mostly intact washroom was just down the hall, he returned to his mate.

She didn't stir as he hastily barricaded the office door, too. The single high window had already been boarded up, probably by the owners of the factory shortly after war broke out, so he was able to relax a little.

It was by no means a satisfactory nest, but it would do for now.

Henrik's kohl-darkened hands trembled as he unclipped his sleeping mat from his pack and laid it out on the dusty floor. She felt as delicate as spun glass in his clumsy hands as he arranged his mate on it.

"You're safe now," he assured her, falling onto his haunches. Twining their fingers together, he leaned his aching back against the cold wall and finally let out a slow exhale of relief.

She couldn't hear him, but he still promised her, "I'll build us a fire in a moment, my blessing." A soft laugh escaped his rough throat. "It'll be our first Burden's Moon bonfire."

He rested his head against the wall. A smile pulled at his lips. As soft as a breath, he whispered, "What a gift."

The Darkest Night: Sugar and Snow 2

Mabel came to consciousness to the sound of a crackling fire and a deep voice singing an old, sad song.

It'd been a long time since she dreamed, so she didn't dare move a muscle for fear that the softness of it would dissolve under her fingers like candy floss. She couldn't remember the last time she'd been truly warm, but it didn't matter because she was toasty down to the thick wool socks she'd been assigned when she was conscripted. That sort of thing only happened in dreams.

Small comforts like warmth and a soft bed were foreign to her now. They were as intangible as memories of home or the taste of sweet things, and she did her best not to think of them. It only made the day to day of her work harder.

Life was hard enough as an entire battalion's only healer.

No, don't think of that, she sternly instructed herself. *The dream will end and then you'll be back in the guts and piss and misery.*

She forced herself to relax her muscles one by one and listen to that deep bass voice. The crackle of flame was a soothing accompaniment to what sounded like a knife skimming wood. It was a familiar rhythm her father practiced every night as he whittled all sorts of things for her mother. The *schwick* and *thwit* of a knife carving wood had been her lullaby until her father's arthritis slowly put a stop to it.

But in the dream he was still carving, apparently.

Mabel let out a sigh of contentment. She didn't want to wake up in her threadbare cot and triage more men. Death clung to her in long trailing ribbons, making every new day and every tiny movement more laborious. One day she was fairly certain she'd simply stop functioning altogether as the weight of all those ribbons bore down on her.

Maybe this is it, she mused. *Maybe I've died and this is what Grim's riverbank really looks like.*

It wouldn't be so bad if that were the case. She was awfully tired of war, and if she got to rest—

The sounds of carving stopped. So did the sad song. Before she could begin to find that odd, a massive hand settled on her brow. It was heavily callused and warm as it stroked the fine hair back from her forehead. Magic lurched from the deep, burning core of her soul to meet that hand in an explosion her flesh barely contained.

"Easy, my blessing," an impossibly deep voice rumbled. "All's well."

Mabel's eyes shot open.

Hovering over her, limned by golden firelight, was the most terrifying orc she'd ever seen. He was nearly twice her size in every possible measurement. Dressed in a battleworn Orclind Iron Chain uniform, she could've identified his rank from across a battlefield.

Between bruises and lacerations, the orc's skin was a pale slate gray. His hair, long around his ears and swept back, was a slightly darker stone color streaked with silver. His size and coloring were striking, but in the firelight all she saw was his eyes.

They were a stunning hazel. Deep forest green flecked with chocolate brown stared down at her from behind a thick fringe of black lashes. The fire glittered in them, giving his eyes a gem-like quality she'd never beheld in another being before. Not even the shifters, whose eyes *did* change color, managed to look so... ethereal.

She'd never been so close to an orc before — except, of course, when they were trying to kill her.

All at once, the situation presented itself to her as it truly was. This was no dream. She wasn't back in her family home, laid out on the chaise while her father carved a new spoon for her mother.

They'd been ambushed. Her triage tent had been blown apart just as she was assessing a cougar's amputated leg while another man groaned in the final throes of a gangrenous infection beside him. There was smoke and death and freezing mud and—

A massive orc charged her with a bloody warhammer raised, a roar ripping from his powerful throat that rivaled explosives going off all around them.

This orc.

Mabel shot upright with a scream. The orc's eyes widened as he reared back, massive hands raised in the universal gesture of peace.

"Wait, please. I'm not going to hurt you," he soothed.

Mabel might've been a naive farmgirl once, but not anymore. She'd done her training in the big city of Minneapolis. She'd lived in a dormitory. She'd been the battalion's only healer for nearly a year. She'd been around the block, as they said, and that meant she didn't believe a word out of this soldier's mouth.

Scrambling backward, she kicked off an unfamiliar wool blanket and a heavy soldier's oilskin jacket. Her head pounded with the echo of a wound her abilities had already taken care of, leaving her even more disoriented than she already was.

When her back met a cold plaster wall, she glanced down and discovered with horror that her uniform was gone. Her bloodied pinafore, sleeve covers, and headscarf were also gone.

All that was left to her were her combinations. The beast hadn't even left her stays.

Face turning a violent red, she pressed herself flat against the wall and hissed, "Is this what the Chain does to their prisoners of war? Strips them to their skivvies?"

The orc leaned back on his haunches. Rubbing the back of his neck with one hand, he bleated, "You were soaked through with mud and... other things. I worried you'd catch a cough."

"Oh, certainly!" Dragging the blanket up to her chest, she drew her shoulders back and demanded, "Take me to your commanding officer, sir!"

The orc winced. "Ah, my blessing—"

"I have rights! I'm a prisoner of war and a healer. I demand to speak to your commanding officer— and— and to be given suitable clothing!"

Mabel looked around, but instead of the tent walls or cell bars she expected to see, she was alarmed to find what looked like an abandoned office. A heavy secretary desk had been pushed against the door and a fire had been built in a rusted metal vat.

"Wha... What is this?" She drew her knees up to her chest as her alarm grew. "Where's the camp?"

"This isn't a camp," the orc answered. "You're not a prisoner."

"What do you mean this isn't a camp?" Mabel pressed the blanket to her throat. It wouldn't do anything to shield her from the hammer-wielding maniac in reality, but having it was better than sitting there in her underthings.

The orc let out a noisy exhale. Shuffling backward a bit, he stood up slowly and walked toward the fire. "Here," he muttered, snagging a canteen off a makeshift grate over the barrel. "You need to warm up. I've made some tea for you, and I've got some rations for you to eat if your stomach can take it."

"Answer my questions," she demanded, voice pitched high.

The orc ambled back over on his massive booted feet. He was obviously wounded, with blood seeping through clumsily applied bandages beneath his uniform, but he didn't appear to care. Kneeling next to the bedroll, he held the canteen out to her by the frayed strap.

Instead of answering her, he said, "My name's Henrik. What's yours?"

Mabel stared at the steaming canteen with a deep dread. "Mabel."

"Mabel," he rumbled with far, far too much pleasure. "That's a very pretty name. Please drink some tea, sweet Mabel."

Heat rose to her face in a different sort of way when he looked at her like he did then — all pretty eyes and a soft smile. Pale fangs peeked out just above his lower lip when her hand lifted without her permission. Their fingers brushed.

She was so shocked by the thrill that brief contact inspired that she looked at his hand, which must've had some sort of magical ability she'd never encountered before.

But no, it was just an ordinary — if comically large — orcish hand. A kohl-black, iridescent hand.

Her mind halted like a cart's wheel catching a rut in a road. Before she could get it moving again, Henrik rumbled, "You're not a prisoner and I'm no longer a soldier. We're mates, my blessing."

He was very lucky she didn't have the stomach to kill him.

Mabel tightened his oilskin jacket around her body as she huddled against the wall. Henrik, the orc who'd kidnapped her, sat in a chair by the makeshift stove, knife and stick in hand. He was clearly pretending not to notice her scrutiny, but he wasn't doing a very good job. Every few seconds his eyes would flicker in her direction before fixing back on his whittling.

He'd tried reasoning with her. He'd tried reassuring her. He'd tried to explain that it was totally normal for an orc to snatch his mate, and it was even *more* normal for him to barricade them in an office.

She didn't believe a damn word out of his mouth.

But escape wasn't possible. Even if she could move the heavy mechanical equipment he'd put in front of the door, it only took a peek through a gap in the boards over the windows for her to determine they were thoroughly snowed in.

"I'll make dinner soon," he informed her in that rolling rumble.

The butterflies in her belly were deeply vexing. Almost as much as him holding her captive. "I don't want your dinner."

"I'll make it all the same," he replied, unruffled. "It's a mate's job to provide."

Mabel's chin jutted. "I don't want a mate, either."

"And yet you have one, just as you'll have dinner." He flashed her a smile full of lower fangs. "The gods know what's best for you and have delivered it without you needing to ask."

"Witches don't have their mates thrust upon them," she corrected him. "We *choose.*"

Henrik nodded. Setting down his small knife and whittled stick, he laid his hands on the desk he'd turned into a table. He gave her a very serious look when he asked, "And have you chosen?"

Her face pinked. "That's an awfully impertinent question."

"Is it?"

"Yes. We're strangers, and you're an enemy besides."

Henrik gave her a long look. "We're not strangers. We're clan now. I ought to know if there's a man out there I'm stealing you from."

Indignant on behalf of her imaginary suitor, Mabel stood up from her spot on the sleeping mat. "Sir, if I *were* married or bonded, I can assure you, no one would *ever* be able to steal me from them."

The orc leaned back in his chair. It creaked ominously under his considerable bulk as he gave her a slow, satisfied smile. "Aye, that's a good answer, my blessing."

Her blush deepened. "What's your plan, orc? Drag your new mate back to your superiors and conscript me into service? I bet you'll get a fine commendation for that!"

Henrik pushed himself away from the desk. It didn't take an experienced healer to catch the sharp wince that briefly tightened his features as he stood, let alone the fresh bloom of blood that stained his shirt.

Giving his head a small shake, he summoned a smile. "As of this moment, my plan is to feed my mate and make sure her nest is warm. I suspect it will be much the same tomorrow."

Mabel tried to maintain her glower as she watched him turn toward the stove, but it wasn't easy watching his face drain of color like that. Every small movement seemed more difficult than before, and the sloppy dressing on his wound raised her hackles.

A bad dressing or improperly cleaned wound meant infection. Infection meant gangrene. Gangrene meant death — if you were lucky.

A healer could work miracles, but once infection set in, they were little better than the butchers who called themselves surgeons.

She didn't need to heal the orc. He'd kidnapped her, after all, and absconded with her to only the gods knew where. Even small battlefield wounds could prove fatal, but he was a big, strapping man. He could, and likely *had,* survived much worse. Not to mention the fact that healing him was technically treason.

But when he had to brace a hand on the wall as he put pressure on his bandage, she couldn't do *nothing.*

Rubbing her eyes, she wrestled with her professional pride and her loyalties. She lost. "Henrik," she sighed, "sit down."

Straightening quickly, he assured her, "I'm fine, my blessing. I just needed a moment."

"No, you need healing." Forcing her boots across the floor, she gestured toward his chair. "Sit."

He turned toward her. For a moment, he seemed unsure about whether she meant it or not, but when she met his questioning look with a raise of her eyebrows, he sprang into action. Or as much as he could under the circumstances, anyway.

Henrik fell back into the chair with a muffled groan.

It was normally the easiest thing in the world to quiet the part of her that was Mabel in favor of the part of her that was a healer. She'd been trained ruthlessly by the head healers in Minneapolis to set herself aside — mentally, physically, emotionally — to care for her soldiers. On the battlefield, there was no room for delicate sensibilities or proper manners. Whatever maidenly squeamishness she'd once possessed had long since died.

And yet, when she ordered him to strip, she felt... unprofessional.

Mabel's breath caught as he revealed a slate gray chest roughly the size and firmness of a brick house. Blue-black tattoos swirled across his shoulders and over his chest, and the flesh covering the sturdy cage of his ribs bloomed with dark green and violet bruises. His shoulders and upper arms were relatively undamaged, but she still struggled to look away from them, which was... unusual for her.

Gods knew she'd seen every inch of men before. A thick orcish chest wasn't particularly noteworthy.

Definitely not noteworthy, she reminded herself with a firm internal shake.

Ignoring the heat in her cheeks, she tried to set aside the curious way her heartbeat refused to slow and examine her captor.

Brows drawing together, she asked, "How long have you been fighting, soldier?"

Henrik shot her a wry smile. "That bad, hm?"

"I've seen the like of it," she answered, reaching out to palpate a nasty, knotted scar on his chest. She did her best to ignore the way his muscle rippled under her touch. "Soldiers who've been in the field too long without a healer all tend to look a bit like a quilt."

In a quieter voice, he replied, "You're the first healer I've seen in a long time."

"That's because most of us are dead." Rolling up the long, long sleeves of his oilskin jacket, she used only the tips of her fingers to peel away the edge of his bloodied bandages.

Even sitting, Henrik was nearly the same height as her. When she leaned in to place a hand over the nasty shrapnel wound on his side, it brought their faces uncomfortably close together. She could count his eyelashes if she wanted to. Which she didn't.

"Mabel." His hand closed over hers, stalling her work. Peering into her eyes, he rumbled, "When I saw you on the battlefield, the gods spoke to me. They told me to find mercy, to protect you at all costs. Perhaps I've seen too many dead healers and taken one too many hits to the head, but I heard them all the same. You're safe with me — not simply because I'm your mate, but because it's my duty."

Her throat tightened. "I don't believe in the gods anymore, soldier. No god would allow the horrors I've seen."

Lifting her hand to his lips, he pressed a soft, reverent kiss to her knuckles. "The gods guide us even in the darkest night, my blessing."

Slipping her tingling fingers out of his grip, she whispered, "The night's lasted a very long time."

"Aye," he replied, settling his hands on his thighs, "and now that I've found the light again, can you blame me for wanting to protect it at all costs?"

The Brightest Lights: Sugar and Snow 3

He understood why Mabel was upset. He just wished she would stop trying to escape.

"My blessing," he sighed, gently extracting his mate from the vent she'd crawled into when he was distracted, "you must stop this."

"Let me go!"

"I can't do that," he replied, dropping her onto her wee booted feet. Wiping a smudge of gods only knew what from her silky cheek with the pad of his thumb, he gave her a good once-over to make sure she hadn't injured herself somehow. "We've talked about this. It's too dangerous, and with the snow—"

"I could be saving lives," she argued, as intimidating as a fluffed up kitten. "Instead you've got me locked up in a damn sugar factory!"

He'd lost count of the number of times they'd had this conversation over the last week. There were many things he'd learned about his mate while they were snowed in, but chief among those things was that she appeared to be primarily composed not of flesh but determination.

Directing her away from the half-caved in factory floor, Henrik gave her soft backside a gentle pat. "You won't be saving any lives if you're dead, and that's exactly what will happen to you if you run back to the front lines."

Mabel shot him a scarlet-faced scowl over her shoulder. Her dress hadn't been salvageable, but it'd been a battle all its own to convince her of the fact. It took two days for her to warm up to the small boiler suit he'd found in the locker room. It was a damn good thing, too, because he *loved* watching her walk in it.

And now that she'd gotten more comfortable with him sneaking small touches, it was all he could do to distract himself from getting his greedy fingers on her.

Swatting his hand away from the curve of her backside, she muttered, "You don't know that."

"I do," he replied, suddenly serious. "Trust me, my blessing. I do know that."

Her shoulders rounded. Rubbing her eyes, she sighed, "I'm sorry."

"You have nothing to apologize for," he assured her. Trying to lighten the mood a little, he nudged her toward the office, where they'd set up what he called their nest and what *she* called her cell. It was a fun game they played.

Smiling down at his witch, he added, "Except, perhaps, for making me burn our dinner."

Mabel perked up instantly. "You found something?"

"While you were busy crawling through vents like a wee mouse, I found a cellar in one of the houses nearby. There was a family of raccoons living in the—"

She stopped abruptly. He nearly jumped out of his skin when she grasped his sensitized hand, gripping it tight. Her eyes were wide when she asked, "You didn't kill one, did you?"

"Uh..." It took a moment for him to think past the shock of her touch. It wasn't often that she touched *him*. Giving her time to adjust was crucial, but that didn't mean smothering his urges was easy.

Something not helped by the lack of a proper nest, he thought, the beast of his instincts clawing at his insides.

Giving himself a stiff internal shake, he answered, "No, my blessing. I won't be making that mistake again anytime soon."

He winced at the memory of their first week, when his rations ran out and he'd proudly presented her with a bird he'd managed to snare. It'd been a very long time since he spent any time with a healer, so it didn't cross his mind that she might be horrified by the thought of eating meat.

It tended to come alive a little on the tongue, apparently, so he could hardly blame her for wanting nothing to do with it.

It didn't make providing for her any easier, but Henrik set himself to the task without complaint. It was a privilege to take care of his mate, and it sure as fuck beat day after grinding day on the battlefield. Even sleeping with one eye open to be sure she wouldn't try sneaking off in the night, he couldn't remember the last time he slept so well or felt so full of life.

"Well, good," she replied, pert little nose sticking in the air. He hid a smile, knowing that meant she was feeling a little soft toward him and leaning hard on her armor.

As they neared the office, Henrik hurried ahead of her to open the door. He did it because even decades of soldiering couldn't wipe out the lessons his clan taught him — but also because her face went all pink without fail.

The fact that it made such an impact on her made him sad, but he couldn't complain about the results.

Ushering her inside, he closed the door to keep in the warmth. It'd taken some serious engineering, but he'd managed to rig up something like a stove out of an old metal drum and a chimney by routing pipes through a hole in the ceiling. They'd taken apart just about every bit of wood furniture they could find and used it as fuel, and the more the room warmed, the heavier the scent of sugar became.

The smell was in the walls. It crusted every barrel and bit of rusted equipment. It was dark and a little burnt, but it was far better than the shit he'd been smelling on the battlefield. If he never got a whiff of gunpowder or blood again, he'd be a happy man.

And their little home, imperfect as it was, beat the tar out of any encampment.

They'd turned a desk into a table of sorts, which sat near the stove, and at the far end of the room was the nest. Which he hadn't been invited into yet. Unfortunately.

Henrik slept on a mat closer to the fire — and the door. Seeing as his blessing still occasionally tried to scamper off back to near certain death, he'd set to guarding it. But those attempts had fallen off somewhat over the last week, which he took as a good sign.

Even today's attempt felt a little half-hearted. She'd made an awful lot of noise for someone so desperate to escape him, but he wasn't about to point that out.

Mabel settled into her usual seat at the makeshift table with a sigh. He moved to the stove, where a tin that'd once been destined for beet sugar now bubbled with beans and canned carrots. There wasn't much in the way of seasoning available, but salt did a lot when the only other choice was nothing.

He felt her gaze on him as he carefully ladled out some stew into his soldier-issued tin bowl. She watched him often with that keen, witchy gaze, probably searching for things he couldn't understand.

Mabel had a tricky brain. She was smarter than him by leaps and bounds, and despite the fact that she had no trouble speaking her mind, she tended to keep a lot of what went on in that sharp mind a secret.

One day he intended to unlock all of those secrets, but for now he'd settle for a smile or two.

Setting his bowl and a far nicer one he'd scavenged from a house in town on the table, he eased into his seat. "Can't beat beans and carrots," he announced, flashing her a smile.

Mabel looked at him for what felt like a long time before her gaze dropped to her stew. She was quieter than normal as she picked up her spoon and began to eat. His mate was a talker, which he appreciated even when she was railing at him. Henrik loved the sound of her voice and just how damn clever she was.

Sometimes, when she wasn't fighting to stay mad at him, she told him all sorts of interesting things — plots to books they didn't have available in the Orclind, or what it was like to be able to see inside a body with her hands, or even stories from her apprenticeship days. She filled their nest with color whenever she opened her mouth.

But she was silent as they ate.

Henrik's appetite dwindled as the quiet stretched on. Instinct prickled. They'd been getting on well, all things considered, for the past week. To suddenly have her behavior shift back to what it'd been those first days made him wary.

"You all right?" he cautiously inquired.

Mabel pushed her stew around with the back of her spoon. "Yes," she answered, not looking at him.

"Really? Because you'd normally be done with your supper by now."

She shot him a quick narrow-eyed look. "You saying I eat too fast?"

"Not even a little. If anything, you could stand to eat more and faster." Pushing his bowl away, he crossed his arms and rested them on the table. "You'll eat better on my homestead. When the weather clears some, we'll—"

"I can't go with you," she sighed.

Trying to restrain his growing frustration, he argued, "You say that, but we both know it's not true."

"It is," she insisted, suddenly all agitation and energy. "I swore to do my duty. As did you! How can you be so comfortable abandoning your cause, Henrik? You act like you're a man of morals and principles, but how can that be true when you're willing to just walk away—"

"From what, Mabel?"

He had a lot of patience, and he was willing to fight with his mate until Grim ushered in the end of days, but one thing he couldn't stand was her dedication to a cause that saw her as little more than meat for the grinder.

Henrik leaned forward a little, trying with everything in him to impress on her the truth of what he said. "Whatever *cause* existed once at the heart of this war died a long time ago. For gods' sakes, Mabel, you were *born into it.* You've never known a life beyond it. I'm telling you that more exists off the battlefield, but you won't get to see a bit of it if you go back."

Her chin wobbled, but his stubborn, beautiful mate firmed it enough to bite out, "And what about you?"

"What about me?"

"You volunteered," she argued, "you chose this life. And now you want to abandon your men? All for what?"

"For *you,*" he snapped. "My orders — the entire Orclind army's orders — are to capture or kill healers, Mabel. And it's not just us. It's the shifters. It's the elves. It's the dragons. You're too dangerous to be allowed to stay with an enemy, and the fewer there are, the bigger targets you become. I've put my time in. I should've retired from the front lines a decade ago, but I didn't because I didn't know what else I was good for. But now I do."

Her eyes were glossy in the firelight, and when she spoke, her voice was husky with unshed tears. "And what's that?"

Instinct compelled him to reach across their table and draw her into the safety of his arms, but he restrained himself. They'd been arguing circles around this conversation for two weeks. It had to be out, to be done, for them to truly find their footing.

Swallowing hard, he answered, "Protecting you."

Mabel looked away quickly. In that raw voice, she breathed, "Henrik..."

"No, you gotta hear me," he insisted, at last giving in to the clawing need to reach across the table to grasp her perfect, powerful hand.

Nearly growling the words, he confessed, "You're worth a thousand of me, Mabel. I've done nothing but take lives that ought not've been taken for too many years. I'm drowning in regrets, and Grim will count them all when I meet her at the riverbank. But this fool war won't change because we aren't there to fight it anymore. It'll keep grinding on, chewing up folks like us, until the day there's just no one left. You can't tell me you don't see that. And you damn well can't tell me you truly *want* to go back to that life."

Her fingers curled around his. They shook a little, but they held on tight as her eyes closed. The fringe of her lashes glittered with tears in the firelight when she admitted, "I hate it. I'm... I'm so *tired* of not being able to save people."

His heart broke for his poor mate. It was unnatural, crushing a healer under the weight of so much death. They were the stuff of life. Not being able to save those in their care would be a fate worse than death for creatures crafted by the gods to heal.

Still holding her hand, Henrik got up from his chair and circled the table. Kneeling by her chair, he brought her knuckles up for a lingering kiss. "You've done your best, my blessing. That's all anyone could ask of you."

"But don't you see why that means I have to go back?" Her eyes opened, revealing so much conflict and pain. "If— if I'm capable of saving even one life and you don't, that makes me a killer."

His nose wrinkled with a snarl. "Tell me, how many lives will you save if you die on a battlefield tomorrow, Mabel? And how many lives will you save if you *live?* If you abandon the meat grinder and find ways to help the suffering that won't end up with you blown to pieces? There are civilians who need you. Babies. Soldiers too wounded to fight. There is more to this war than the front line, my blessing."

Pressing his lips to her knuckles again, he murmured, "I'd never ask you to stop healing. All I'm asking is for you to live."

Her index finger slowly uncurled. Brushing his cheek, she whispered, "And you'd help me do that? Save other people? You just met me."

"I would," he answered, thrilled to his bones by that gentle touch. "Because you're my mate, my blessing, my light in this terrible world. The gods gave me a gift when they picked me to guard you, Mabel. I intend to cherish it."

She said nothing. Her eyes, so bright and uncanny in the flickering light, darted back and forth as she examined his face. Whatever she found there must have moved her, though, because she leaned down slowly.

He held his breath, afraid that even a sigh might scare her off. His heart hammered as she brushed her lips against his — a chaste kiss that tasted like sugar and magic that made the world go bright.

Too bright.

Magic was a bomb blast between them, as hot and devastating as any ordinance, and within a few heartbeats, the world fell away, as dark as the winter solstice itself.

Light the Way: Sugar and Snow 4

The journey to Henrik's homestead wasn't an easy one. Pavilion, the closest town to his land, was at least a week's journey during fine weather, but they weren't favored with that. And of course, the war raged on.

Their first major hurdle was getting safely away from the front line. The weeks of blizzards had done wonders to quiet the worst of the fighting near their sugar factory, but that didn't mean it was safe. The border between the Packlands and the Orclind was fuzzy at best and littered with minefields at worst.

To make things more perilous, shifters had subterfuge on their side. They could change into animals at will, which allowed many of them to lay in wait for enemies. Any hawk could be a scout, and behind any corner a battalion.

Unfortunately, that meant the safest course of action was to go through the wilderness, which was no easy thing in the middle of January.

They did their best to prepare. The abandoned shells of homes were scavenged for anything useful, and Henrik fashioned her a pack out of a sack that once held sugar beets. She was in charge of the blankets — or nesting materials, as he called them — while he shouldered the cooking supplies, wood, and makeshift tent he'd rigged up with an old tarpaulin and whittled posts.

He was a remarkable man, her orc. Mabel was as awed by his resourcefulness as she was by his restraint.

Despite taking the kohl and her surprise bonding, he continued to be the perfect gentleman. Or near-perfect, anyway. The man did have an unbecoming obsession with patting her backside.

They'd shared a bed ever since she dragged his unconscious body into it, but he hadn't taken the opportunity most men would've. The soldiers she knew were desperate for female company, and the few times her shifters had stumbled their way into a matebond, desire ran hotter than a furnace. She'd been under the impression that orcs were similar, but Henrik never slipped his hands inside her combinations or did more than bestow dizzying kisses.

In some ways it was a relief. It took time for her to come to grips with what he asked of her, and now what her magic had decided for her. She was attracted to him, to be sure, and she was a healer. She knew the mechanics of the intimate act. There was nothing to fear about it other than, perhaps, the compatibility of their sizes.

But she was nervous all the same. Perhaps that was why he restrained himself.

Her bondmate was a perceptive man. Sometimes it felt like he spent all his time watching her, learning every expression and variation of her voice. There was no way he hadn't seen her blush or look away quickly when he stripped for bed.

And she could allow that perhaps he was focused on more important things than sex.

After the elation of her bonding died down, Henrik grew intensely fixated on getting them back to his homestead. The man hardly slept. He worked furiously, gathering supplies, crafting what they needed, and trying to outfit her with every bit of clothing he could find.

When they set off, the soft, charming orc she'd come to know fell away to reveal the hardened soldier he'd been forged into.

"You must follow every order I give you," he firmly instructed her as he adjusted the high collar of his oilskin jacket around her face. His expression, normally cheerful, had settled into deep lines of determination and worry.

But he wasn't the only one who'd been fighting too long. Mabel knew how to follow orders. Nodding, she replied, "Understood."

"And if you get tired or too sore, speak up. We'll be in a far worse position if you injure yourself than if we stop for a break."

"I've marched before," she explained, shifting a little under the bulk of the layers he'd piled onto her. "I can keep up."

"Even so." Henrik bent to give her a gentle kiss. A rush of tingles spread from her head to her toes when the tip of his tongue swept across the seam of her lips. Pulling back with a strained look, he muttered, "If it would get us to our nest faster, I would carry you."

"You're awfully focused on nests," she observed, knowing her cheeks were bright red.

The powerful muscles that lined Henrik's jaw flexed. Skimming his palm down one side of her head, he sighed, "You have no idea."

She didn't understand what he meant by that until many nights later, when they retired to their tent. A light snow fell outside, forcing them into the great hardship of cuddling close beneath their blankets to conserve warmth.

They were both fully dressed, exhausted, and a little filthy from the journey, so it wasn't exactly the time for romance. But Mabel couldn't take it anymore.

Pressed against his chest, she couldn't see his face when she demanded, "Do you not desire me?"

Henrik tensed. "What?"

"You haven't... I mean, I know what mates do," she said, painfully glad he couldn't see her expression. "And I'm your mate.

You're a soldier who hasn't... known a woman in a while, presumably. But you haven't touched me. Do you not desire m—"

"Have you lost your mind?" Henrik's growl shook the very air beneath their blankets.

Before she could react, he'd flipped her on her back. The blankets slid down over his shoulders, letting in a waft of frigid air as he loomed over her, a furious scowl on his face.

"Listen to me. No, better yet—" He grabbed her hand and dragged it down his front, to the closure of his trousers.

"Do you feel me, Mabel?" he rumbled, pressing her hand into the hard bulge beneath the layers of wool and undergarments he wore.

Her face flamed. A heavy sort of feeling settled into the pit of her stomach. It was warm and rich and exhilarating.

It was desire in its purest, most intoxicating form.

"I..." Mabel swallowed hard. "I feel you."

Ignoring her soft sound of protest, he pulled her hand away and set it back on their sleeping mat. Henrik lowered his head to press his lips to the pounding pulse below her jaw. She gasped at that soft touch, the spark of her own magic singing in her veins.

Being bonded was an odd, remarkable sort of thing. She'd never given it much thought, being too young to consider it and then too wrapped up in death to see it in her future. But her body had chosen for her, and what a man it picked.

Henrik, who crossed a battlefield for her. Henrik, who believed his mission was to help her help others. Henrik, who wanted nothing more than to see her thrive.

It was overwhelming at first, and a part of her still struggled to come to grips with it, but after three weeks locked together, she *knew* him. And she liked him. She liked him very, very much.

Whispering into her skin, he told her, "I desire you, my blessing. By all the gods in the sky, I desire you more than I can take. But I've made a promise to myself that I won't touch you until I can give you a proper nest."

Thoroughly distracted by the way he kissed her neck, it took her moment to catch up.

Blinking rapidly, she gawked at the dark ceiling of their tent. "What? Why would you do that?"

"Because I will *not* take my mate for the first time on a floor, or in a tent, or anywhere except the home she is owed." Henrik skimmed his lips over her jaw to murmur in her ear, "We will stay in the homestead to rest, eat, and fuck until we have our fill of it all."

"Oh," she squeaked, toes curling in her thick socks.

His lips curled into a smile against her skin. "And I'll be sending in my declaration of matehood to the commander of the Iron Chain Forces. No one will drag me back to the fight when I have a mate in my nest."

Filled with a strange mix of relief, disappointment, and desire, she wrapped her arms around his back. Chest tightening, she asked, "You won't be arrested, will you? For desertion?"

"No," he assured her. "Matehood is sacred. If they court-martialed every orc who ran off with a mate, they'd have a revolt on their hands."

Searching his uncanny eyes, she dared to ask, "We'll be safe?"

"Yes, my blessing," he answered, touching his forehead to hers. "We will be safe. And then we will work."

The homestead was of traditional orcish design, just as he'd explained it to her as they walked for days and days.

But even his vivid descriptions couldn't prepare her for the loveliness of it.

Snow dusted a sprawling, sloping field and the round structure that made up the turf roof of the main house. Walls of stone only about three feet tall stuck out from the earth, while the rest of the home was buried deep. A short flight of stairs led to a heavy wood door, and a spindly iron chimney stuck out of the turf roof like a broken arm.

Tucked deep into orcish territory, it was miraculously unscarred by the war. To Mabel, the peace of it was almost painful to behold.

Henrik led her down the steps by the hand. He'd boarded up the door during his last mandatory leave period, so he pried them off with his massive, kohl-darkened hands before he unlocked the door with a heavy iron key.

Ushering her inside, he hurriedly explained, "I built this homestead, but when my parents pass, we'll inherit their ranch in Colorado. It's much larger and on a good trading road. I figure... well, when we have children, we can give one of them this place."

Mabel stood silently as he pulled her sugar beet sack off her back and set it on the floor. Her gaze roamed the lovingly decorated space, taking in the tapestries on the walls and the hand-carved furniture. The air was slightly musty, but the temperature was startlingly comfortable. It felt more like a home than anywhere she'd been in... years.

Henrik was all movement and nervous energy. He dropped his own pack before running to the iron stove in the middle of the round living room.

"I'll get the fire going to heat up some water for a bath," he babbled, shoving kindling into the belly of the stove. Striking a long match against the flagstones, he asked, "Do you like it? The house, I mean. It's fine if you don't. I can change whatever you want, and the nest is—"

Mabel knelt down behind him. Wrapping her arms around his middle, she pressed her face between his shoulder blades. "It's wonderful," she whispered. "It's so, so wonderful."

Henrik sat back a little on his heels. Covering her hands with one of his, he sighed, "Good. It's yours now."

Summoning her courage, she whispered, "I know you're exhausted, but..."

"But what, my blessing?"

"Will you share the bath with me?"

Henrik sucked in a deep breath. In a rough voice, he answered, "Aye, I will."

They were both worn down after weeks of perilous travel and close calls, but none of that mattered. Henrik fetched a massive copper tub and set it up in the middle of the living space before he went off to bring in water from an enclosed well off the kitchen. Mabel found soft linens for drying and a large pot for boiling.

As the room was warmed by the roaring fire, so were they by the desire that simmered between them.

With every pot of steaming water they poured into the tub, the anticipation grew.

"You should get in first," she offered, suddenly self-conscious.

Henrik nodded, but he didn't begin to strip right away. Instead, he stepped around the steaming copper bath to settle his hands on her hips. "Let's undress together," he suggested. "That way we're equal in this, as we are in all things."

Mabel looked up at him. Her throat was tight with nerves when she whispered, "I've never done this before."

"Aye, I guessed." He stooped to press soft kisses to her cheeks and brow, tracing a path down to her lips. "There's nothing to fear. What we do or don't do, all that matters is that we're together. If all we share is a bath, I will be happy."

Mabel turned her head slightly, desperate to keep his lips and breath and skin near. "How do you have so much patience for me?"

"Because," he whispered, fingers beginning to gently pull apart the layers of her scavenged clothing, "I've known the worst of the world. When the best stands in front of me, what complaints can I have?"

Her breath caught. Henrik's hands, so callused and scarred, were careful as he slowly undressed her. Steam from the bath kissed the skin he exposed, and then so did he.

By the time he'd discarded his own clothing, her worries seemed small and unimportant. They certainly couldn't stand up to the image of him, as tall and broad as a mountain, standing nude before the fire.

Slate gray skin criss-crossed with scars stretched over thick slabs of warrior muscle. Those swirling tattoos drew her eyes to the mass of his shoulders and chest. A faint trail of dark gray hair trailed down from his strong stomach to draw the eye to a heavy, erect cock framed by muscular thighs sprinkled with hair.

A finer specimen of a man did not exist in the world, and he held his darkened hand out to her.

Henrik climbed into the hot water before he guided her to settle in front of him. She was acutely aware of him against her back, and the length of that cock pressing urgently against her backside, but he wasn't in a rush. He stoked her desire with gentle touches and exploratory swipes of the washcloth. He scrubbed her hair and ran his claws through the tangles, smoothing out the snarls until it ran in a smooth, wet curtain down her back.

When it was his turn, she took a deep breath and stood up. Water sluiced down her body, its path followed by hungry hazel eyes, before she sank back down into the warmth — straddling him.

Henrik grunted, his hands settling onto the soft flesh of her hips and backside, as the ridge of his cock found its way unerringly to the wet warmth of her cunt.

Chest rising and falling with rapid breaths, she began to wash him, too. But it wasn't like the hundreds and hundreds of baths she'd given patients. There was no clinical separation.

There was only appreciation and the marvel of him, her Henrik, who allowed her the time to learn him at her own pace.

Mabel carefully shielded his eyes from the water she poured over his hair, rinsing out the soap she'd scrubbed into his scalp. When he was clean of suds, she dropped the cup onto the floor and stroked his jaw. Her thumbs brushed water from his cheeks and brows in reverent swipes.

"Thank you for saving me," she murmured, rocking her hips a

little. Friction, delicious and forbidden, sent a shock of pleasure up her spine.

Henrik's hands snaked between them. They cupped her damp breasts, gently squeezing and rolling her pert nipples, then moved down. His fingers slid across her trembling stomach before they found the slick skin of her cunt.

"I've done nothing except return the favor," he rumbled, stroking the bundle of nerves she was so used to touching alone in the dark of night. Her eyes fluttered closed as her hips rocked into his hand, seeking more.

Henrik's fingers swirled, gliding through water and her own wetness. She could feel him watching her intently, but even if she couldn't, she would've known. His cock, huge and hard and hot against the entrance of her body, throbbed with every pass of his fingers.

Curling the fingers of his free hand around the back of her neck, he dragged her down for a deep, probing kiss. Speaking into her mouth, he growled, "I'll have one release before we leave this bath."

Mabel dug her fingers into his shoulders. Her magic hummed beneath her skin, a melody of contentment that grew louder and louder as the tension in her belly increased. Henrik wasn't rough with her, but he was relentless. His fingers never grew tired or missed a beat. He pulled an orgasm from her with terrifying skill.

Her shoulders curled and her cunt clenched hard as it rolled through her. The aftershocks hadn't even begun before Henrik's growled and swept her into his arms. He stood up from the bath, carelessly splashing water across the stone floor.

Nude and dripping, he carried her down a short hallway to another room she barely saw. Stars still glittered in her eyes when he parted heavy curtains to lay her in a strangely shaped bed.

Her body, lax and wet and full of buzzing desire, wasn't prepared for the lips and tongue that found their way to the juncture between her thighs. Mabel's back arched clean off the bed as his tongue found her clitoris at the same time that his finger slid inside her.

It was a storm of sensation, one of pleasure and slight discomfort as he soothed her with his mouth and stretched her with his fingers. Another orgasm hovered just out of reach, lurching closer and then backing off as he worked, until he tightened his lips around her with a hard, sucking pull.

A sound like a sob escaped her, interrupted only by the shock of him slowly pushing the broad head of his cock inside her.

Her limbs wrapped around him, holding tight. The discomfort of his size was astonishing. It blended with the ripples of her powerful orgasm, confusing her body until all she could do was cling to him.

"Easy," he whispered into her hair. His big hands cupped the top of her head as he slowly flexed his hips, testing their fit. "I won't move until the pain eases. Just breathe, my blessing."

Mabel buried her face into his damp chest. The smell of him, clean and earthy and *hers,* filled her lungs. For the first time in years, she felt more than alive. She felt *embodied.* Like she was more than Mabel the healer. She was Mabel the blessing, the woman, the lover who was flesh and blood and raw, bodily wants. It was the most miraculous feeling she could imagine.

"Keep going," she ordered, stroking her hands down his muscled back. "I want to feel you, my mate."

Henrik's groan reverberated through her. He seemed incapable of a response, but she didn't need one.

He pressed forward, making a home for himself between her thighs, until she swore she could feel every ridge and vein of him molded into her flesh. The first stroke was a shock. The second made the muscles of her thighs twitch and shake. The third…

The third dropped her mouth open.

Mabel gasped, shocked by the feeling of fullness and electricity that accompanied every roll of his powerful hips. It was a bizarre feeling, being full of him and massaged from the inside, but it was a joyous one.

Sweat beaded on her freshly cleaned skin. It wasn't just hers. Henrik's chest rose and fell like a bellows as he thrust. To keep her from sliding up the bed, he eventually sat up on his knees and lifted her hips to meet him, changing the angle so the flared head of his cock stroked the front wall of her channel with every roll of his hips. The sounds of their bodies meeting was loud and wet in the confined space, heightening the pleasure of every tiny movement.

A silent cry left her as she clawed at the bedding, her cunt clenching sharply down on the monstrous cock shuttling inside her faster and faster until he slammed home with a deep groan.

A foreign warmth filled her as released inside her. Mabel's legs tightened around his hips instinctively, trapping him there as he rode out the waves of his orgasm.

Henrik slumped over her, panting and sweaty. Finding her lips with his own, he breathed, "I intend to love you for all my life, Mabel."

Draping her weakened arms over his shoulders, she sighed, "It'll be a long life, won't it?"

"Yes," he whispered.

Mabel smiled against his lips. "I intend to love you all our life, Henrik. All our good, long life, come what may, and beyond it, too."

END

Splintered Vigil: Chapter One

CONFIDENTIAL

18 January 2041

An assessment on the psychological state and recommendations for the members of Fracture from Dr. M. Starsbury, M.D. submitted by request to the Sovereign's Office:

On 2 June 2040, I was given the assignment to assess the mental and emotional wellbeing of the members of the special Patrol unit known as Fracture by General Valen Yadav. These members were Vesta Kincaid, Sloane Fortuner, Arjun Donovan, Lucien Prince, Johanna Titus, Arlo Downing, and Cesare Runeare. My assessment took place over the course of six months, during which time I conducted interviews, inspected their living quarters, examined their backgrounds, and shadowed them when their assignments allowed.

This brief should be considered an overview of my findings. A report on each member, as well as much more thorough recommendations, can be found in the attached report.

The objectives of the assignment were split into two parts. The first was to determine whether the members of Fracture (hereafter referred to as "subjects") could be adequately rehabilitated and reintroduced to independent life amongst the civilian population. The second objective depended on the findings of the first. Should the subject(s) be found unfit to return to the general populace, I was asked to recommend the best and most humane course of action for their future.

OVERVIEW:

Under proper supervision and with intensive support, the subjects are not a danger to themselves or others. Without supervision or support, the subjects represent a viable threat to the health and safety of the population of the Elvish Protectorate.

OBJECTIVE ONE:

After six months of intensive study and deliberation, it is my professional opinion that none of the subjects can or should be allowed to live unsupervised amongst the civilian population. This is not only for their own mental and emotional stability, but for the safety of the populace.

All of the subjects have endured horrors and conditioning the likes of which most people would not survive. As elves taken from their families, some as young as three, and raised by a rotating squad of Thaddeus II's most brutal and war-damaged hitmen, they lack the fundamentals of basic communication skills, emotional intelligence, and compassion. It is my belief that many of these things can be taught, but given their many years of conditioning and service, they will never achieve what most would consider "normal" behaviors.

When asked what they would do should they be released from their service, none of the subjects had an answer. Even the suggestion of living an independent life seemed to unsettle them, and in a few it even sparked outright aggression.

Socially, they appear to have developed a unique pack-like structure with two "alphas" at the top: Vesta Kincaid and Sloane

Fortuner, who seem to split authority evenly and defer ultimately to their Captain, Kazimier Rione. These bonds are not built on what most people would view as warm, familial relationships, but a mutual understanding and codependence. In my time with them, I observed many instances of what I can only label as silent communication between the subjects. Their understanding of each other is so complete that it is rare that they truly need to speak, and when they do, they tend to express themselves through clipped speech and strategic bursts of violence.

OBJECTIVE TWO:

After determining that the subjects cannot at this time or in the foreseeable future be released from supervision, I turned my focus to finding the healthiest path forward for the team. While my list of recommendations is long and involved, the most important point can be boiled down to one vital conclusion: If the government wishes to see the subjects live semi-independent lives, the members of Fracture CANNOT and SHOULD NOT be split up for any reason.

Although nearly all of the subjects (notable exceptions being Downing and Prince, see p. 57, subtitle CODEPENDENCE) are extremely independent and exhibit striking anti-social behaviors, they heavily rely on the pack structure of the team to regulate their emotions and validate their experiences. Although they may often seek solitude, they would never under normal circumstances wish to completely cut themselves off from the pack.

It is my belief that should a subject do so, it would represent a dire mental and emotional state in need of immediate intervention. At the time of my assessment, I saw no indication that any members of the team wished to live on their own. They appear to be aware that their stability depends on their coexistence.

However, I have grave concerns over how that dynamic will change when any of the subjects find their mates. Not only will it cause immense emotional and psychological upheaval — as it does in all elves — it may threaten the fragile support system that keeps every member of the team regulated. Broadly speaking, the subjects have no capacity to handle the emotional turmoil, arousal, possessiveness, jealousy, or territorial urges that come with the critical period of bonding.

It is my expert opinion that the members of Fracture should be shielded from any possibility of finding their consorts until such a time that they are deemed capable of handling the changes both on an individual level and as a group. All necessary precautions should be taken and a plan put in place for the dangerous possibility that those precautions might prove inadequate.

It is well known that all elves go through a period of dangerous instability when they find their consorts. For the members of Fracture, it would be more than dangerous. It would be catastrophic.

OCTOBER 2047 — San Francisco, The Elvish Protectorate

Killing wasn't the point, but it was always a pleasure.

Sloane enjoyed hunting. Whether it was for an assignment or for his extracurriculars, he never tired of it. He had no memories of what it was like to play as a child, and only a bare bones understanding of what civilians found pleasure in, but a lifetime of training had wired the idea of a successful hunt to satisfaction. The pounce and the kill — they were as close as he came to knowing happiness.

He got a lot less of that these days.

After she beheaded her father and took over the territory, Delilah's changes took a long time to reach them. The rest of the territory needed immediate stabilization, and they'd served her faithfully in the shadows. But when the dust cleared and it became obvious that a bloody civil war had been avoided, it was their turn.

They'd been called Thaddeus's attack dogs. The terror in the dark. The shadow squad who could find anyone, anywhere, and leave a bloody message for all the world to see.

Now they were a liability.

What did one do with attack dogs when they were no longer needed? Put them down.

So it came as something of a surprise when instead of taking them out, a wave of psychiatrists, mind healers, and specialists were brought in to "make reforms." New luxuries were brought into the Fracture barracks. New doctors assigned to each member. New rules were strictly enforced.

They weren't expected to maim, torture, or kill anymore. Not unless their lives or those of civilians were directly threatened. For the first time since Thaddeus snatched them from their families, they were given the gift of mercy.

They had no fucking idea what to do with it.

The team wasn't fit for domestication. They couldn't be assimilated or softened. They certainly couldn't be expected to know what to do with *kindness.*

Each of them had adapted to the unsettling change in circumstances in their own ways. They found hobbies, *extracurriculars,* that scratched the itch their assignments no longer did. For Sloane, the team's premier assassin, it was hunting.

He left the barracks without a word. Consistent good behavior had gotten him the privilege of freedom when off duty. It was another new luxury he and the rest of Fracture exploited to the fullest extent.

Sloane rarely had a plan for his hunts. He didn't need one. The Elvish Protectorate was one of the most strictly controlled territories on the continent, but even it had its seedy underbelly, injustices, and violence behind closed doors. He rarely had to search long to find someone the world was better off without.

On this particular foggy October night, however, he wasn't having a lot of luck.

Tension bunched the powerful muscles between his shoulder blades as he vaulted over the top of a chain link fence blocking off an alleyway. Elves valued cleanliness above just about anything, since their heightened senses made them particularly affected by powerful smells. That meant that their streets were cleaned nightly by automated bots. The same couldn't be said for alleyways, where elves rarely ventured.

Luckily for Sloane, his full-face helmet filtered out scent. Cutting off one an elf's most powerful senses seemed counterintuitive for a group raised to be hunters, but the loss was worth it. Their sense of smell was a powerful tool, yes, but it was also their greatest weakness. One whiff of the right person at the wrong time...

Of course, not smelling the rot of trash, piss, and discarded food behind a bar was nice, too.

Sloane had to rely on all his other senses to find his prey. His breath whispered out through the helmet's filter as he landed in a crouch on the other side of the fence. His boots, steel-toed and laced high up the shin, flexed comfortably as he stabilized on the balls of his feet. He scanned the alleyway.

Besides the thump of bad music inside the bar to his right and the flash of headlights from passing cars at the exit of the alley, there was little of interest.

Fuck, he thought, gloved hands curling into tight fists. He hated going back to the barracks without a catch. It was the only thing that kept him going through the mind-numbing monotony of their new, sanitized assignments. Getting a good kill in, wiping one more stain off the face of Burden's Earth, stopped him from losing what little of his mind he still possessed — and taking out all the pent-up aggression on his teammates.

The last time he failed, he and Arlo sparred so intensely they'd both ended up in Joanna's clinic with half their bones broken. The repairs to the gym were *still* coming out of their pay.

But it was more than just a need for release. It was about a tangled knot of purpose and thwarted instinct, a result of all that malicious rewiring Thaddeus and his trainers had labored so intensely over. Without the hunt, he was useless. Purposeless. A weapon with no edge and no enemy.

To return to the barracks unsuccessful was, in his mind, worse than failure. It meant that he'd failed his only purpose in life.

The bar was his last hope. The sun would rise soon, and that meant that the Haight district would be flooded with vampires headed home for the day. Not all of them, just like not all of the business that was conducted within the confines of The Lush, were criminal in nature. But he'd had luck there in the past, so he figured it was a good final stop of the night.

A low metal groan drew his attention to the bar's back door. The thumping beat of the music grew louder as it opened. A small yellow light flickered to life above the frame with the motion, casting a watery glow over the figure that slipped out.

"...next week! I'll let you know if my schedule changes!" A chipper, feminine voice was the last thing he expected in the dank filth of the alley.

Sloane didn't move a muscle as he waited for her to step out from behind the door. A chorus of voices called out to her, wishing her goodnight before she let the door swing closed behind her.

She was willowy, with lithe limbs and a head of long raven hair. Her skin was a deep olive tone that looked silky to the touch. When she stood there for a moment, her focus on digging in the glittery purse slung over her shoulder, he had what felt like all the time in the world to observe the soft curve of her nose and sooty fan of her lashes against the tops of her cheeks.

She was arrant. He knew it at a glance, something inside of him flinching instinctively away from the devastating vulnerability of her. To someone like him, everything about her was almost perverse in its softness.

One painfully delicate hand rummaged in that ridiculous purse, the bones of her wrist flashing beneath the sleeve of her pale pink sweater with every movement. So much smaller than his. So easy to snap.

Elves had eaten humans, once. They'd eaten pretty much anyone weaker than them, and no one was weaker than arrants — those poor humans born without even the flimsy protection of magic.

To Sloane, this pitiful little creature looked like a doe, blissfully unaware of the wolf hiding just out of sight.

Something pulled inside him; a deep, sucking sort of feeling he couldn't easily identify. It wasn't anticipation and it wasn't quite hunger. It was some foreign mix of both and neither — a need that had no name, no predecessor, and no equal.

She wasn't prey. Not the kind he sought, anyway. And yet she was something he needed to possess.

The woman stood in that dim light for several long moments, tapping away at her phone. Her lips, shiny with some sort of makeup, were set in a soft pout. The cool light from her phone's screen reflected in them like a beacon.

The more he stared at them, the worse that nameless need became.

A wild kind of anger sparked to life as he watched her, like her helplessness and ignorance were a personal slight. How could she not sense him there, crouched mere feet away? Had she even bothered to look around the alley before she stepped out? Didn't she realize what an elf could do to her with barely any thought at all?

Their bones were harder than concrete. Their claws had a molecular structure similar to diamonds. Their upper and lower fangs were self-sharpening and could come together with a bite force great enough to bend steel. He was a predator unlike anything else on the planet and she was...

Beautiful.

Sloane blinked, taken off-guard by the thought. As far as he could remember, he'd never used the word in his life. There hadn't been any reason.

But when she tucked her phone back in her bag with a soft sigh and brushed her hair back behind her ear, it was the only word that made sense. She was beautiful. Something in the way her features were put together and the softness that radiated out of her like heat off blacktop made her that way.

Sloane reared back, sinking further into the shadows as he examined the strange creature. To him, she seemed like something that came from another world. The reasons why wouldn't come to him no matter how hard he tried to drag them out.

She wasn't any different from the thousands of people he'd encountered — and hundreds he'd killed — in his lifetime. A human was a human. An elf was an elf. Everyone could be killed, so no one was special.

She wasn't even doing anything interesting. He doubted she was on her way to commit a crime. Going by the short black dress under the pink sweater and the fact that she used the employee exit told him she was likely a server just getting off work for the night. There was nothing, *nothing*, noteworthy about her at all.

But he followed her.

When she walked out of the alley in her tennis shoes, a hum in her elegant throat, he was right behind her. The reasons why continued to evade him but they mattered less and less with every step.

It took him a block to realize what he was doing, and only after a man passed a little too close to her for his comfort.

Protection duty.

His boot nearly hit a discarded can as he quickly dipped into the shadows between buildings, his gaze locked on the slim shape of her back and swaying hair. He'd never been allowed on a protection assignment before. Those were given to Vesta and Cesare, who liked people best, or Arlo and Lucien, who were inseparable and required unique assignments. No one, not even their new, progressive captain, would consider Sloane fit for a job that didn't require killing.

But he followed her. And he was pretty sure he didn't want to kill her.

Sloane's vision narrowed until all he could see was the shape of his prey. The sense that something terrible was going to happen to her, that if he looked away for even a moment she'd be taken from him, was overwhelming.

His blood rushed in his ears, nearly blocking out the sounds of the street that filtered in through his helmet's speakers. It felt hotter than normal. Brighter. Like he'd been injected with something that made him feel... more. Bigger.

So when she turned a corner into another dark alley, clearly intending to cut time on her walk, it was a shock to feel something in his chest lurch. The fine hair on the back of his neck prickled with unease.

She clearly didn't hear the shuffling footsteps at the other end of the alley or have the honed instinct to detect threats that he did. Something was wrong. Something was waiting. For the first time in his life, the urge to reveal himself not to kill but to protect nearly overwhelmed him.

Sloane abandoned his cover just in time to hear a high, nervous laugh.

"Oh, Cole! I didn't see you," she exclaimed, too far away.

When Sloane entered the long, narrow alley, he found a reedy man standing over the doe, one hand clasped on the softest part of her upper arm. Neither appeared to notice their audience when the man replied, "Your blonde friend wasn't working tonight. I figured you'd need some company walking home, so I caught up with you."

"That's really nice of you, but I don't think Roxanna would be too happy if she knew you were walking other girls home, Cole. Best you should get along, huh?" The cadence of her voice changed. It slowed and sweetened, reminding him of the way he'd heard some people speak to their pets or bawling young.

Sloane walked slowly, the tread of his boots silent on the cracked concrete. That needy, aching thing in him began to beat at the underside of his sternum — a steady *thump, thump, thump* to match his footsteps.

"C'mon, Cece," Cole whined, "she won't know. She's been too busy for me, anyway."

"I'm sorry to hear that, but I really need to get home." The woman, *Cece* — such an odd, pretty name for an odd, pretty woman — moved to step around Cole.

Several things happened at once: the man grabbed her arm to yank her back toward the dingy brick wall, Cece yelped, and Sloane moved.

Fighting and killing were muscle memory. Blinded, bleeding, and impaired by a severe head wound — it wouldn't make a difference. He'd fight entirely on autopilot and win, because losing hadn't been an option since he was six years old.

His reaction to the sight of a man grabbing *her,* however, was something altogether different.

It wasn't autopilot. It wasn't even instinct. It was a sudden and explosive severing of a nerve, that essential mechanism that kept him so tenuously tethered to basic decency.

One moment he was standing in the shadows, watching a hand close around her pink-swathed arm, and the next his own hand held the back of Cole's head against the gritty brick and mortar. A watery scream escaped the man's throat as the delicate bones and cartilage of his face gave way under the pressure.

Sloane didn't hear any of it. Flames engulfed his senses. His fury was the kind that could only be described as *scorched earth,* a feeling so all-consuming that it destroyed everything it touched.

Until someone touched *him.*

SPLINTERED VIGIL

THE NEW PROTECTORATE FRACTURE BOOK ONE

ABIGAIL KELLY

Splintered Vigil: The New Protectorate Fracture: Book One

Finders keepers.

Sloane knows he shouldn't watch her. A predator trained from childhood to do what no one else will, his specialties are murder, mayhem, and torture. He's a danger to just about everyone, including the soft human woman he stalks day and night.

Losers get a bolt in the head.

Cecilia Warren is soft, sweet, and blessedly ignorant of the bloodshed he deals in — until the day she's attacked. The plan is to save her, not keep her. But everything goes awry when he finally gets her in his claws. Instincts blur loyalty. Desire makes letting her go impossible.

If they want to take her, they'll have to kill him first.

The mission objective shifts when he goes from protector to captor, secreting her away and going AWOL from the terrifying shadow unit known as Fracture. They have orders to hunt him down and free Cecilia against her wishes. Sloane won't give her up and he won't back down, even if that means destroying himself to protect the only good thing he's ever known.

Pre-order Splintered Vigil now!

Also by Abigail Kelly

Find all new releases, short fiction, comics, bonus chapters, and exclusive content on the Works by Abigail Patreon!

Grim's Delight: The New Protectorate Syndicate: Book One

A bloody war nears its end.

Felix Amauri is the rightful heir to the most powerful vampire crime family on the continent. After years of taking out challengers to his claim, everything he's fought for is finally within reach — until one sloppy assassination threatens to ruin everything.

To be human is to be prey.

For years, the worst thing Dahlia McKnight could picture was becoming a vampire's toy. She never imagined that she'd witness a brutal assassination, let alone that she'd be turned in the process. One day she's a waitress, the next she's the sole heir to a vicious crime family embroiled in a war of succession and the target of an icy vampire prepared to do anything to take what he's owed.

He needs her for more than just her blood.

Learning to be a vampire is hard enough, but when it's discovered that she can carry another vampire's offspring, nothing will stop Felix from claiming her. If she wants to be more than just his plaything, it'll mean becoming the predator she was born to be.

Glossary

A full character directory and map can be found at Abigailkkelly.com

Places

United Territories and Allies: What we would consider the continental USA. A loose federation of sovereign states established after the Great War. The UTA capital is United Washington, in the Neutral Zone.

The Elvish Protectorate: Also known as the EVP. Stretches from Oregon to New Mexico. Capital city is San Francisco. Led by the elvish sovereign Theodore Thaddeus Solbourne and Margot Goode.

The Coven Collective: Also known as the Collective. Encompasses Washington state. Capital city is Seattle. Led by a large coalition of witch covens, with Sophie Goode acting as their leader.

The Orclind: Encompasses much of the Midwest. Led by the Iron

Chain, a close-knit government made up of orcish clans and Queen Sigrid Seagrim. Capital city is Boulder.

Shifter Alliance: Takes up a section of the midwest and all of the south. (Unfortunately includes Florida.) Run by a very, very loose alliance of shifter packs from three capital cities — Minneapolis, Oklahoma City, and Atlanta. Unofficial leader is Lee Seymour.

The Draakonriik: Also known as the 'Riik. The second smallest territory, it takes up all of the Great Lakes region and stretches to New York. Led by Taevas Aždaja, the *Isand* (ee-zand) of the dragon clans. Pronounced: *dra-kon-reek*

The Neutral Zone: Also known as the New Zone. Technically it is held by a coalition government consisting of representatives from the UTA, but in reality it is run by a syndicate of feuding vampire families. It is a small strip of land squeezed between the Draakonriik and the Shifter Alliance.

Gods

Light & Darkness: The primordial gods who created all the others. Also known as The Lovers and First Union. Both are generally represented as female.

Loft: God of the sky and creator of flying beings. Twin sibling to Tempest. They know no gender. Also known as the Boundless One.

Tempest: God of the ocean and creator of all water beings. Also known as the Hungry God and the god of love.

Burden: God of the Earth, creator of all beings who live within it — most notably the orcs. Husband of Glory.

Glory: Goddess of sunlight, magic, and creator of elves. Worshipped by witches for giving the gift of magic to humanity.

Blight: God of forested places and disease. He works in partnership with his daughter Grim and shares her dominion over demons and all reviled creatures.

Grim: Goddess of death. Known as the Merciful One and the Brilliant Lady. She is widely beloved.

Craft: God of change, newness, and messengers. Creator of humanity and viewed warily by non-worshippers as the Chaos Maker. They change their gender frequently, but generally is referred to using he/him pronouns.

TERMS

Alpha: a broad term used by many communities generally associated with a leader — either of a small family group, a pack, or even a territory.

Anchor: a vampire's mate. Anchors are carefully chosen and usually longterm-to-permanent arrangements, as they take considerable energy to make/become. A vampire must inject their venom into a host many times before their blood chemistry adjusts such that they become unsuitable for consumption by another vampire and their sleep cycle switches to a nocturnal pattern. At this point, they can also produce/carry to term a vampiric child. Temporary anchors do exist, although they are relatively rare due to the intense withdrawal symptoms associated with ending the regular venom intake.

Arrant: someone born without m-paths, or the ability to channel and use magic.

Burnout: the colloquial name for the degenerative medical condition caused by excessive magic in humans. Over time magic can damage nerves and brain tissue, which will inevitably result in death if not treated with development of a witchbond.

Change: an elvish term for a sudden shift into adulthood. This is marked by 5-14 days of "madness", usually triggered by some stressful event around the age of 16-18. The elvish body is flushed with hormones to the point where sudden growth, overwhelming hunger, and aggression take over. Viewed as an incredibly vulnerable time, only immediate kin are charged with the care of their loved ones — which includes isolating them, preventing harm to themselves/others, and feeding them. The change marks the second phase of an elf's life, when they are no longer coddled children but young adults who can accept challenges and family responsibilities. Formal adulthood is attained at 30.

Changeling: a term first used to refer to fey children fostered out to non-fey homes, now more widely used to mean any person raised by people who are not the same beings. *Ex:* A dragon couple raising a human child.

Chosen: the formal term for a dragon's mate. The act of finding a mate is called *Choosing,* and is considered sacred.

Consort: an elvish mate. A term used exclusively by elves to refer to someone they are biologically compelled to pair up with. This usually involves intense sexual attraction, but can vary from person to person.

Demon: a being with horns or antlers, pointed ears, and symbiotic shadows. They are generally considered to be some of, if not *the* toughest beings in the world, as their shadows can make them almost indestructible. They are also naturally extremely strong and durable. Demon clans tend to be extremely close-knit, partially due to the fact that the world at large is not wholly accepting of them and their mythological connection to the god Blight. Identifying mating features are utter devotion, heightened protectiveness, and the sharing of shadows. This is when a mate is "given" a piece of the demon's symbiotic shadow, which will then live on that person for the rest of their life.

Dragon: a person with a dual form. In their bipedal form, they have claw-tipped wings, horns, and a tail. In their quadrupedal form, they are roughly the size of a standard SUV and can fly at extremely high altitudes for weeks at a time. They come in a variety of extremely saturated colors that shift with the time of day (light to dark). They breathe cold blue fire and can see the Earth's magnetic field. Identifying mating feature is marked change in behavior, including the overwhelming urge to nest.

Elemental: a being created by a spontaneous magical eruption. They often take on the attributes of whatever weather they happen to be born into, *i.e.* a lightning storm might produce a lightning elemental, or a blizzard might make a snow elemental.

Empath: a person with the ability to feel and manipulate the emotions of others.

Elf: someone born with jewel-toned skin, claws, pointed ears, and four fangs. Very secretive and considered apex predators who require a strict hierarchy to function. Average height of 6-7ft. Identifying mating feature is the retraction of claws.

Fever: shifter mating imperative triggered by the "animal's" choosing of a mate. Marked by a perpetual near-shift — elevated body temperature, increased aggression, build-up of magic, and the compulsion to mark. A shifter displays their readiness to find a mate by creating a den.

Fey: a person with nearly vestigial, insect-like wings, small fangs, and claws. Usually live in large groups. Identifying mating feature is bioluminescence.

Foresight: the ability to see multiple possible futures. The average number is between 2-4, with the likelihood mental instability increasing with each subsequent possible future.

Great War: a conflict between the territories of the North American continent that began in 1817 and ended in 1917 with the signing of the Peace Charter, which established the United Territories and Allies of modern times.

Halfling: the elvish term for an elf with mixed heritage.

Harpy: a being with bird-like wings and talons for feet. They live in family units called flocks and prefer to build nests high off the floor with access to open air. Culturally, they believe that aggression and competition are marks of a well-adjusted person. They are monogamous and fiercely possessive of their mates.

Healer: a person who possesses the ability to see into and heal bodies through touch.

Isand: the title of the leader of the Draakonriik. Pronounced *ee-zah-nd*

M- : M- is frequently used as shorthand to denote when something is infused or otherwise combined with a magical element.

Marriage Sigil: a custom symbol branded into the foreheads of spouses (pairs or multiples). Each one is unique and infused with a small amount of magic as a reminder of the power love holds. They are typically sought out by worshippers of Glory — mainly witches and arrants. Elves, though worshippers, don't usually take a marriage sigil when they find their consorts or form a unions with other elves.

Mate: a catchall term for a significant other. Used by many cultures, it has varying degrees of weight. To shifters, orcs, and demons, the word mate is synonymous with family, monogamy, and dependence. It is much more loosely used within arrant society, as well as amongst elves, who generally prefer the term *consort.*

Merfolk: a catch-all term referring to sentient beings who live in the ocean, lakes, or rivers. Due to the nature of the ocean and its inhabitants, classifying all beings individually is almost impossible, so a much broader term is used to refer to both mammalian and non-mammalian beings than would be used for those on land.

Met: acronym for *magically enhanced tech.* A branded home assistant that can do everything your Alexa can, as well as small, low-level magic to help around the house.

Metallurgic Inoculation: a vaccine given to all elves within hours of birth to make them immune to iron poisoning.

M-siphon: a containment device used to imprison a magical being and siphon off their magic. Highly illegal.

M-lev: a play on *maglev,* meaning a high speed train that levitates using magnets. In this case, magnets *and* magic.

M-weather: magic weather. Very common, but can result in "clusters" or storms that wreak havoc if not properly contained. In rare circumstances, it can also produce a sapient being known as an *elemental.*

Nymph: a person who possesses a symbiotic mycelium that allows them to communicate with plants, hibernate beneath soil, and access the collective memories and experiences of those in their family line. Every nymph is part of a network known as a *hyphae,* and all hyphae are connected to the original.

Orc: a person with green, gray, russet, or blue skin, two fangs, and claws. Widely renowned for their strength and beautiful voices. Identifying mating feature is "the kohl", or altered, dark pigmentation of the hands and feet developed after meeting their mate.

Pixie: a small, winged creature with compound eyes with about the same level of intelligence as a rat. In the wild they live in trees and in burrows, but have adapted to living in walls, pipes, mailboxes, etc.

Pull: elvish mating imperative. A sudden hormonal shift caused by exposure to a compatible partner's pheromones, marked by the retraction of claws and volatile mood shifts. The pull is only "satisfied" when hormone binding occurs — the term for long term exposure to a mate, resulting in permanent biological dependence on their pheromones. This process increases fertility and often results in the conception of multiples. Lack of exposure to a mate can cause severe physical reactions (lack of appetite, muscle pain, headaches, insomnia) as well as the deterioration of mental stability.

R-siphon: also known as *reverse siphon.* New technology that redistributes magic away from the siphon instead of into it.

Shifter: a person who can shift into an animal form. They can partially shift (changing only parts of their bodies at will) and often take on characteristics of their other half. Famous for their strength and tenacity, as well as their dual-voiced "shifter purr" which many people find deeply attractive. Usually found in packs.

Sigil: a symbol used to channel magic. Western countries use the alchemical alphabet formally codified in the 1800's, though many, many variations are used all over the world.

Sovereign: the title of the ruler of the Elvish Protectorate. It is capitalized when used in place of a name.

Turbo Virgin (c): Theodore Thaddeus Solbourne, Sovereign of the Elvish Protectorate and Head of the Solbourne Family.

Union: an elvish marriage. Usually done for financial, political, or procreational benefit. The parties involved are not fated or biologically compelled to be with one another, and might have many lovers or even a consort outside of their union.

Vampire: a person who drinks blood to survive and cannot go out in sunlight. Vampirism can only be "caught" with the exchange of fresh blood, and as of 2045 is much more widely spread through procreation. Vampires can only breed with their *anchors.* Identifying mating feature is marked change in behavior, including overwhelming desire and need for total isolation.

Ward: a magical barrier with varying levels of protection. A ward can be something as simple as a proximity alert — "someone walked into my garden" — or as complex as full on defense — "someone crossed the threshold and has now burst into flames". The severity of the ward depends on the complexity of the sigils used to create them, and wards can have many layers, each one with a unique purpose. Personal wards can also be used, such as in clothing or embedded into jewelry, though they tend to be expensive and difficult to foolproof.

Were: a person infected with the were virus, a much mutated strain of the vampirism virus, resulting in altered physiology and magical ability. They can be identified by their heterochromia, or different colored eyes. They are the newest magical race and viewed warily by the general public for a variety of earned and unearned reasons. Identifying mating feature is marked change in behavior, including highly increased territorial instinct and the urge to nest. Pronounced *ware.*

Witch: Humans with the ability to use magic, which is passed down genetically. A person needs to be born with m-paths (a unique nervous system) to use it, however, humans were not initially adapted to use magic safely. Geneticists believe they acquired the ability through interbreeding with other beings. This interbreeding resulted in many unique qualities, such as the massive variety of abilities, power levels, and unique skills known to select families. However, it is also responsible for "burnout", which is the degenerative neurological condition a witch with mid-to-high level power will experience if they do not share their magical load with another being via witchbond. Witches are classified from least to most powerful — brightling, brilliant, and gloriana.

Witchbond: a magical bond formed between a witch and another being. Due to the nature of magic and humanity's much more recent adaptation to it, witches of *brilliant* and *gloriana* power must form a bond with another being usually beginning around 150-200 years old. This bond filters magic through the other being, neutralizing its damaging effects and reducing the chances of burnout to almost none. This bond also gives a power boost to the partner. A witchbond is permanent and can only be severed if one of the partners dies, at which point the surviving partner can form a new bond. Though commonly associated with a romantic partner, a witchbond is not inherently romantic and can be shared with a friend, sibling, or (ill-advised) an enemy.

Wraith: sentient shadow beings not dissimilar to elementals. They can affect the world around them in small ways, but can only speak to a very small number of demons. They lack physical forms but those that fully develop have complete sentience, personalities, and desires.

About the Author

Abigail Kelly is a writer and illustrator of alternate histories, love stories, and women with drive. Her work is heavily influenced by both her modest family roots and her passion for history. Her favorite authors are Shirley Jackson, V. E. Schwab, Ursula K. Le Guin, Kresley Cole, Nalini Singh, and just about anyone who writes about the weird and wonderful.

She lives in San Francisco with her dog, Babs, who remains stubbornly illiterate.

Content warnings

Pregnancy, alcohol, experiences of war, blood, pregnancy, non-graphic vomiting, medical care, estranged family, PTSD, and explicit sexual content.

www.ingramcontent.com/pod-product-compliance
Lightning Source LLC
LaVergne TN
LVHW010655110826
845149LV00014B/3101

* 9 7 8 1 9 5 7 8 4 4 1 7 6 *